KNAME'S BOOK

James Gregory

Buried Treasure Books— Collinsville, TX
ISBN: 978-0-578-75639-4
Library of Congress Control Number: 2020916613
Title: *Kname's Book*
Author: James Gregory
Digital distribution | 2020
Paperback | 2020

This is a work of fiction. The characters, names, incidents, places, and dialogue are products of the author's imagination, and are not to be construed as real.

Dedication

Raya, life is measured in years, but defined in moments, thanks

Prologue

March 28, 2018

Olivia crossed the Arkansas line into Texas and pulled into the Texarkana Welcome Center. It was raining and cold for late March. It had rained all of the way through Arkansas. By the looks of the landscape it had been raining forever. She had read where it had been the coldest winter in 55 years in North Texas. She pulled the hood of her sweatshirt over her head as she exited her SUV. Even though she had driven through the rain most of the day, her raincoat was buried in the clutter of the back seat. She didn't want to waste time looking for it. First order of business was to exercise her two dogs. Steele, her male German Pinscher, was riding free in the back seat of her silver Toyota FJ Cruiser. JD, a female Xolo something or other mix was crated in the cargo area behind the back seat. JD was another rescue she took in after her beloved Pitbull Kale died. Every available area of space was taken with clothes, water, food for the dogs and various personal items.

Each dog was leash walked in the exercise area and she contemplated feeding them, but at 4:30 PM she figured she could wait until her next stop. By her calculations she was about 3 and a half hours from her destination. At least one more gas stop and exercise break for the dogs. She checked the water bucket in the crate for JD and offered Steele a drink from a dog bowl. She wiped both dogs dry with a chamois and put them both back in the FJ. JD had been crated most of the trip but there wasn't room enough in the back seat to let them both ride free. Too much clutter, the price for taking too much stuff from Florida. Hard decisions, what to take what to leave.

Then into the welcome center and a quick trip to the bathroom. On her way she gathered a few maps from the collection offered to travelers by staff and received the customary "welcome to Texas" from the women behind the counter. Somehow Olivia thought that she actually sounded sincere, not like it was a requirement of her position.

When she returned to the SUV she checked the cooler on the passenger's seat and grabbed a bottled water. None of the human food that she packed for the trip was left and she figured convenience store snacks would be the best she could do for the rest of the day. She didn't want to stop at a restaurant and leave the dogs in the car alone.

Route 30 out of Texarkana connected to route 82 which runs east and west across the northern most part of Texas. It more or less parallels the Red River which is the Oklahoma border. She ran out of the rain but the clouds still dominated the sky and she marveled at how wide open the landscape appeared. Traffic was light and the patches of drizzle appeared intermittently as the sky was darkening prior to dusk. Small towns and horse or cattle ranches dotted the landscape. Near Bonham she exited 82 and stopped at a Tractor Supply parking lot to feed and exercise the dogs again. She drew an occasional glance from customers in the parking lot, but never feared any harm. Steele weighed about 40 pounds, was 20 inches high at the withers but didn't have an ounce of fat on him. One of her agility friends used to say that he was fierce looking. JD was bigger, stout for a bitch, all black except for a few white spots on her chest and almost scary looking. This disguised her sweet disposition. She made up their food and fed both in the FJ. Then both were exercised, one at a time, on a grassy area adjacent to the parking lot. Both dogs relieved themselves and were situated back in the FJ. Lucky for her both were good travelers.

Olivia wondered what the patrons thought, a few watched her but she didn't feel intimidated. She never owned a gun but knew that ownership was common in Texas. She wondered if having one would make her feel more secure. Not sure, but she figured that taking lessons in fire arms use and safety along with purchasing a hand gun were on her to do list. Not a priority but somewhere on the list.

She cleared Fannin County and entered Grayson County on 82. The clouds and time of day were allowing darkness to set in. It continued to rain off and on. Both dogs were sound asleep as she past Sherman and continued west. She switched from the CD player to the FM band, searching for a local radio station. Lots of C and W, some not too bad sounding. At the sign for Whitesboro she got off 82 and headed south on route 377.

377 was only 2 lanes but after she cleared the intersection leading into Whitesboro the speed limit was 70. Seemed sort of fast for the narrow two lane road. It was dark now but traffic was light and just past a sign that said Collinsville 3 miles she turned left into a gas station / convenience store. She filled the FJ with her credit card and went into the store. Only the clerk was present and he greeted her as if he knew her all his life. He was young, maybe early 20's, not tall but slender. He had a Texas Longhorns faded orange cap pulled down tight on his forehead. Olivia picked out several bags of chips and a six pack of bottled water. She noticed a walk in beer cooler in the rear and decided what the hell, long day a few beers would go well washing down the chips. Inside the cooler the selection surprised her. Oh well she thought, when in Rome, and she grabbed a 6 pack of Lone Star. The clerk

rang up the purchase, bagged the snacks and beer and told her to have a nice evening.

She headed back onto 377 south towards Denton. Her two companions were asleep. Just over the Ray Roberts lake bridge she saw the sign for Paxton Road. Hard left and after two consecutive "s" turns she continued down the country road until she spotted a brick encased mailbox on the right. She slowly approached the drive and through her headlights saw the freshly painted number on the brick, 286. This was it, the house sat back about 200 feet and she slowly drove down the gravel drive. The brick ranch house was dark, but arrangements had been made have the utilities turned on. She pulled up to the garage and sat looking at the house. She stared and wondered if this was the beginning of one journey or the end of another.

CHAPTER ONE

December 7, 2013 1:45 AM

The Quality Inn in Brooksville Florida located on Cortez Boulevard sits right off of the intersection of Interstate 75 and county highway 50. Across from the motel is a Speedway gas station / convenience store, truck stop and a small strip mall anchored by a Winn Dixie food store. A development, Ridge Manor West, sits behind the motel at the end of Cortez Boulevard. Traffic was light save for a few trucks traveling the interstate. It was unseasonably cool for early December and rain showers had passed through in the late night hours. The roads were still wet and a heavy fog hung over the area. The neon lights of the gas station were hard to see in the fog and rain.

The man they call Slider packed his small duffel bag and stored it in the back seat of his rented Ford Taurus. He was between 36 and 42 years old, depending on which set of ID's he carried today. Slightly built, 5' 11" tall, 155 pounds with close cropped thinning blond hair and pale blue eyes that he usually hid behind sun glasses. He wore khaki pants, a plain black t- shirt, a vintage London Fog navy blue jacket and white Adidas cross trainers. He checked his Smith and Wesson model 63 22 caliber revolver and made sure that all eight cylinders were loaded with 22 shorts. Nobody used 22 shorts any longer but they made a clean entrance, no mess and because he used a revolver there were no spent shell casings left behind for evidence. He tucked the pistol into a small holster located on his belt at the back of his right hip. The jacket concealed the holster.

Rather than drive around to the office from his room at the back side of motel he walked around the building and noted that most of the parking spaces were empty. Certainly not a full house. The motel was a former chain motel that was purchased by immigrants from Pakistan. Family members worked at the motel when they got visas and stayed there until they could find other work. The night clerk was a heavy set man of Middle Eastern descent who was most likely related to the owner. He spoke little English, but enough for the night clerk's position at the motel. He seemed overly compliant considering the time of day. Slider noted that there was an old surveillance camera in the lobby, the monitor was visible to him showing a picture quality that was very grainy. He figured it probably only had a 24 hour replay function. Certainly not state of the art for 2013.

Slider paid his bill in cash, took the receipt and glanced up and observed a television behind the counter tuned to a sitcom now in syndication. He walked back around the motel, got into the Ford Taurus and drove east on route 50. There was no traffic and the rain had picked up a bit, the fog made it difficult to see. At the first intersection was a Walmart distribution center access road to the right and an entrance to a parking area for the Trilby nature center and biking path on the left. He drove through the first intersection and continued the crossroads of 50 and route 98. To compensate for the poor visibility he drove slower than usual. He was a patient man, a must in his line of work. The poor weather did have an advantage, it would make any potential witnesses less likely to notice or be able to ID him.

He made a right at the intersection and headed south towards Dade City on route 98. About halfway between the intersection of 50 and 98 and the city limits was Brian's RV Park and Golf course.

Slider had memorized the bio on his target and had watched the park for three days. He never tried to over think his assignment and was never informed of the reason the person was targeted to die. He learned only what he needed to successfully fulfill his part of the deal and then move on as directed by his employer. Although he had never met his employer face to face he always followed his orders and completed his assignments. It was business as usual. Kill him, move on and wait for his next job.

Route 98 between the intersection of 50 and Dade City was mostly rural except for an occasional house, a small mobile home park and neglected former orange groves. There had been a killing frost in the winter of 1984 and many of the groves didn't survive. Brian's RV Park was inhabited primarily by seasonal clients. Most were rich Midwesterners or Canadians that liked to spend the bulk of the winter months in a warm climate. Slider noted that he was the only car on this stretch of road on this early Saturday morning. It was difficult to see the sign because of the rain and fog and he almost drove past the entrance. The drive was composed of a gravel and shell base. He had previously determined that there was no surveillance system in the park. He figured that the residents and the owner probably wanted it that way. He drove the circular drive that was marked one way. He would have to drive all the way around the circle to exit the park. The RV's were evenly spaced and there were two short cul-de-sacs about half way around. One went to the par 3 golf course and the other to the common recreation area and laundry building. There were no lights on in any of the RV's. No

Groover McTuber's awake tonight Slider thought to himself. He passed the office and noted that it was closed. It was still drizzling, Three quarters of the way around Slider pulled up to an older Holiday Rambler RV. He parked just past the RV, exited the Taurus and slowly moved up to the steps. He put on latex gloves and took his lock pick and easily opened the door. Within about three minutes he was back in the Taurus. The only hitch was that the door wouldn't fully close on his way out. The latch was worn and wouldn't fully engage. Rather than attract attention at this early hour, he just left the door slightly ajar. Back out onto 98, still the rain and fog made for a perfect cover. He headed back towards 50 on 98 and then onto the interstate, route 75.

News article in the Tampa Tribune, Pasco County Edition, dated Monday, December 9th, 2013.

Man Found Dead in RV Park

Early Saturday morning officers from the Pasco County Sheriff's Department and the Dade City Police Department responded to an anonymous call from Brian's RV Park located just outside Dade City. Officers discovered the dead body of a man in an RV. A spokesperson for the Pasco County Sheriff's Department indicated that they suspected the victim's death was the result of foul play. The man's name is being withheld pending notification of his next of kin. Anyone having information regarding this incident is requested to contact the Pasco County Sheriff's Department, major crimes unit at 1-800-555-2800 or the Dade City Police Department, criminal investigation unit, at 1-800-555-1400.

Obituary in the Herald Democrat,
Whitesboro, Texas, dated December 16,
2013
William Frederick Kname

William Frederick "Rick" Kname, 62, a resident of Pilot Point, Texas died while on vacation in Florida on December 7, 2013. Mr. Kname was born in East Greenfield Ohio on February 21, 1950. He enlisted in the United States Army in 1968. He served 20 years in the Army which included two tours in Vietnam and a tour in South Korea. He was honorably discharged from the Army attaining the rank of sergeant first class. After his military service he worked for Pacific Engineering as a consultant on military projects. He enjoyed hunting, fishing and watching baseball on television. Mr. Knapp is survived by a niece, Kimberly Wainwright of New Smyrna Beach, Florida and a granddaughter Olivia Kname of Mims, Florida. Services are private. In lieu of flowers donations can be made in Mr. Kname's name to the Vietnam Veterans Memorial Fund.

On December 13, 2013 the man called Slider arrived at the Orlando International Airport with another identification. He turned in a Dodge Charger rental and noted that the airport was particularly busy. The Orange County Convention Center was hosting the 2013 National dog show finals on the weekend of the 14th and 15th. It was a warm December morning and he was dressed in brown cargo shorts, a heather grey pocket t shirt, white New Balance cross trainers, no socks, Oakley wrap- around sun glasses and a navy blue Nike baseball cap pulled down over his forehead. He had a small carry on duffle bag and a Dell 15" lap top secured in a carry case. Slider was able to blend in amongst the curiosity of airport staff, security and patrons as dog handlers and owners moved about securing their dogs in the holding and baggage areas. Slider passed through security without a hitch and waited for his flight to Houston, Texas.

Chapter Two

It was a cold snowy January evening in Burlington, Vermont. The winter of 2016 had been bitter so far. John Price sat in a coffee shop located in the Barnes and Noble book store in the Burlington Mall. He drank coffee and waited for the store manager to allow the patrons in line for the book signing to enter. He looked at the jacket cover of his novel and read the credits, they made him smile and took his mind off of the cold weather and the lineup of mostly middle aged overweight women. He hoped for at least some eye candy. Most of them would ask questions and request personalized messages written in the copies of his book that they had purchased. As long as they bought copies he was fine with the questions and the inconvenience of the signatures. Most of the questions were easy, some irrelevant to the subject matter of the novel. He hoped that there were no difficult questions and if so he figured that he could wing it if asked any really hard technical questions. He had rehearsed possible answers in his mind, after all it was fiction. That was his answer when pressed on issues that he had no actual knowledge of. He would also routinely point out that he did extensive research on the subject and most of his sources wanted anonymity.

The book, The Mind of the Assassin, had been a critical success. It easily made the New York Times Best seller list and it looked as though it was also going to be a financial success. It was the story of a GI whose job was assassinate double agents during the Vietnam War. Price had previously failed at two attempts to get published. One a short novel about a detective on the take and the other a collection of short stories. Neither were very good and other than self- publishing there was no way a publisher was going to pick either one up. He made no money on either and both failed to get his name out there in the world of fiction. Not only were the books not very well received, but the market was shrinking. The less people reading, the more competitive it was to find success as an author.

This book was different. He was surprised at the reception and flattered by the reviews. His publisher and his agent, yes he now could say he had an agent, had insisted on the four book signings. All were in the frigid Northeast, two in Boston, one in Hartford, and now one more in Burlington. All within 6 days. He often dreamed of living in a warm climate where the sun shined more often than not. Maybe now he could live his dream.

He glanced at his watch, 4 minutes to show time he thought. The previous three had been pretty successful and the turnouts above average despite the weather. Only once was he cornered with a couple of questions that he considered difficult. A gaunt looking man who appeared to be in his mid- 60's had managed to wait out the line and cornered Price just as the Hartford singing was closing. The man was dressed in ill- fitting jeans, an old Army field jacket, mud stained work boots and a black watch cap. He smelled of cigarettes and booze and his questions were technical regarding military operations. Price managed to partially answer one or two when he was saved by one of the bookstore employees. She explained that the signing was over and Mr. Price was due at another book store. A lie, but it got him off the hook.

He stretched his legs under the table, took a sip of his Starbucks coffee and waited for the line to start moving. He looked back at the jacket cover and read one the credits to himself. "A tale of brutality in an unpopular war, it almost seems as though Mr. Price was a witness." Hardly, John Price thought to himself, since he was born two years after the war ended.

Chapter Three

Olivia Kname sat in the crating area of at the Orange County Convention Center on December 13, 2015. The crates were assigned by sections and each handler and dog were allowed a predetermined and measured area. She sloughed back in her canvas director's chair listening to the Kings of Leon on her I Phone ear pods. Handlers and dogs were constantly moving back and forth from the staging area for their runs. Small groups of competitors gathered and complained or endorsed the agility courses depending on whether or not they were successful. Twice the music was interrupted by a phone call. She didn't recognize the number and it wasn't a Florida area code. She pressed dismiss and figured she would check for a voice mail message when she got home later that night. Her dog, Steele, lounged in his crate as they waited for their run in the Agility Invitational Finals. She was amazed that she was able to survive the preliminaries on Saturday considering that she was still fairly new to the sport of agility and she and Steele and were struggling to become a team.

Steele was a rescue, another in a long line of discarded dogs taken on by her aunt Kim Wainwright. Somehow Kim had talked Olivia into taking him and seeing if he could be trained to participate in agility. Olivia had only been running a dog in trials for less than three years. She started as a junior handler when she was 16. Her other dog was a pit bull rescue and they had managed to get through the novice level and into open when she got Steele. Steele was younger and more athletic so Kim and Olivia decided she should concentrate on him. She was still considered a novice by most of the other handlers and although she knew many of the other teams by face she was more likely to recognize them by the name of their dogs.

The Invitational was different. There were teams from all over the country and each handler had to qualify with their dog based on an accumulation of points or titles from August 1st of 2014 to July 31st of 2015. Qualifying for the more competitive breeds was difficult, the competition for the likes of Shelties and Border Collies just to name a few was intense. Steele was a German Pinscher, not a breed commonly used for agility, therefore the competition to qualify was less intense. Each breed was allowed 5 dogs for the competition. Olivia was surprised that Steele made the cut for German Pinschers. He was forth on the list and she noted that he was the only one who showed up for the invitational. After all she had only been running him for a little over a year.

Olivia checked the running order and realized that Steele's jump height class, 20", would be up in about 15 minutes. She studied the course map and occasionally glanced at Steele. Many of the crated dogs barked and generally exhibited aggressive behavior. Steele acted as if he could care less. Kim would often say that he only cared about himself. He was easy going and somewhat aloof. He occasionally lifted his head and glanced around, like he was being bothered by the noisy dogs.

Olivia walked up to the staging area and waited for the 8 minute walk through. She was tall, 5'10" and possessed a lean body and although she was attractive she constantly denied it. She wore navy blue Under Armour spandex running pants trimmed in gold. They accentuated her athletic legs. Olivia definitely had the body for spandex. Under her white New

Balance turf shoes she wore grey Adidas ankle socks. On top she wore a loose fitting grey- t shirt and covered her short cropped black hair with a green University of South Florida baseball cap. Some of the other handlers ignored her, especially the women who were not as blessed in the body department. Some obviously shouldn't wear spandex but it was stylish and this was after all the Invitational. She walked the course and made mental notes as to the difficult spots. It was what they referred to as a hybrid course, not one seen in regular competition where points were awarded. It was sort of a combination of a jumper's course and a standard course. The contacts were all included, teeter, A Frame, dog walk but the pause table was omitted. 12 weaves and an assortment of jumps completed the course. It was more difficult than she and Steele had experience with, but it looked fast and that was in his wheelhouse. He liked to run wide open. Tight courses seemed to frustrate him, often causing handler error on Olivia's part. They were both fast, so fast courses went easier for both.

After the standard 8 minute walk through she looked at the running order and noted that Steele was 29th in line. Walking back to the crating area she reminded herself that the course was wide open and would prove to be fast. She said to herself that this was to Steele's advantage as well as hers. She avoided the chatter from the others about the difficulties of the course. She kept concentrating on the positives.

After she returned to the crate, she took Steele outside to the exercise area for a potty break. When they returned she put his flat running collar on him which was blue decorated with red skulls and cross bones images. When she first started to train him she used a flat collar with teddy bears and hearts on it. Kim told her to ditch the collar. "He's not teddy bears and hearts, he's skulls and crossbones." She walked him up to the staging area. Steele was a dark stag red and was perfectly put together. She often got compliments on her handsome dog. He moved almost effortlessly, almost gliding rather than walking. A couple of times over the practice jump and Steele was ready to compete. She spotted her marker dog, the one who would enter the course ahead of her. It was a border collie handled by one of the better handlers. She had heard others talking about them, the team. The handler had a reputation for being condescending. She was good and she knew it. Just before entering the ring she looked back at Olivia and Steele and Olivia felt as though she looked right through her. Steele was unimpressed, he circled around and made eye contact with the border just before they entered the ring. The border and handler were about three quarters of the way around the course when the Gate Keeper signaled Olivia and Steele to the start line. Olivia glanced over and noticed that the border had knocked a bar, a disqualification. Olivia had planned on a two jump lead out, the timer signaled the go prompt, Olivia told Steele to wait and then walked past the first two jumps. She glanced back and smiled, he was ready. "OK Steele, jump."

Chapter Four

Olivia returned home late Sunday evening. It had been a long three days. Instead of staying in a hotel and paying the inflated prices for the room she drove back and forth all three days from Mims to Orlando. It was a little over two and a half hours round trip, she had to leave at 6AM all three days and didn't get back home until after 7PM. Her aunt Kim watched her other dog so she could participate in the Invitational. Olivia worked part time as a title and warranty clerk for a Honda dealership in nearby Titusville. This afforded her the time to participate in training and trialing her dogs. She also worked part time for Kim, who had small boarding kennel on her property in New Smyrna. Kim had raised Olivia after the death of her mom. She got her interested in dog sport and prior to agility she helped Kim who showed dogs in confirmation. After High School Olivia rented a small house in Mims but stayed at Kim's from time to time and continued to help out with the dogs. Confirmation showing bored her and it was way too political for her liking. Agility was different. The people, the atmosphere and the lack of politics attracted Olivia.

Kim stopped by early Monday morning as Olivia was scheduled back to work at noon the same day. It was a sunny and warm morning when she arrived at Olivia's. The drive from New Smyrna to Mims was approximately 30 minutes. Kim was dressed in denim cargo shorts, sandals and white sleeveless button up blouse. She had her long grey streaked black hair pulled back in a ponytail. She entered the house and let Kale off leash. Kale ran up to Olivia, with her tail wagging a mile a minute. It was obvious that Olivia's affection for dogs was genuine, not based on the competition with them.

Olivia and Kim discussed the Invitational over coffee and bagels in the kitchen of the small concrete block home Olivia rented on Dixie Way. Kim was 42 but she looked older. She became involved in showing pure bred dogs as a teenager in the AKC's junior handling program. Kim was a natural and eventually struck out on her own after apprenticing two years for a professional handler.

Bernard Banks was skilled at training and handling dogs and he taught Kim well. But on the downside he was twice divorced, overweight, obnoxious and at times more interested in getting into Kim's pants than tutoring her. Kim absorbed as much as possible in the two years with Bernard but left when hands on was more about him putting his hands on her than tutoring her and showing his dogs.

The years on the road had prematurely aged Kim but she was still attractive and kept herself in good shape. She had recently cut back on clients and spent more time on running her small kennel. That along with a generous divorce settlement from Brian "Sonny" Wainwright set her up pretty well. Sonny Wainwright was a local contractor who got lucky when the Volusia County area became a hot spot for land development. Everything he touched turned to gold. He was good to Kim, set her up well but he also had a roving eye. Sonny and one of his girlfriend's got caught red handed by Kim leaving a Daytona Beach motel. The rest was history. Despite the details and the divorce they remained civil and saw each other from time to time.

"You would have been proud, Steele ran solid all three days. Just missed qualifying on Friday but made up for it Saturday and Sunday. I couldn't believe that we ran so fast and clean to beat on Saturday, both runs. They were both Hybrid courses, both very technical but we nailed it on both. The second run was fast, no real tight turns and I thought it was more helpful for the Borders but he ran great, never missed a Q and was faster than usual through the weaves. I think he ran a 30 and change on a scat time of 41."

Kim looked at her and smiled.

"When I told you to take him I had no real idea if he could be good. He wasn't in the best condition when I got him, you know that. It is a shame he was already neutered, he has blossomed into quite the handsome dog. I could have finished him easily, most of the GP's I've seen at shows are real pieces of shit."

Olivia looked back and teased her.

"Yeah, you breed handlers are all alike, only look at them standing still, you should come to a trial with us and watch him run."

Kim smiled and replied, "you know if I was younger I would give agility a try, certainly takes more skill than showing in breed."

"You're not too old, just too stubborn, plus you got it made with those rich clients of yours, still you ought to come see us run."

"I'm not surprised about him, I was able to find out some informational on his pedigree. His mom was a Swedish import, they breed them for performance over there. I saw a picture of her on the breeder's website, I'll show it to you, she was real pretty. From the pictures I can see where he got that killer rear. The sire is a breed champion and his breeding goes back to the Swedish breeder's stuff. He was shown as a special for a few years, ranked in the top 10, I know the handler. Guy's from Mexico and got into the breed right after the AKC recognized them in 2003. He's a big money handler, not sure but I think the dog's owner had money. Someone told me that the bitch's owner only bred her once and the litter was small. Not sure how he ended up as a rescue, even people who try real hard to screen puppy sales get burnt sometimes."

"Kim, do you think the breeders know he ended up a rescue."

"Not sure, you have his papers, look them up and let them know. I'm sure they are interested in what happened to him, and will like the idea he is being worked. Not sure, but I think they are from the Midwest somewhere, like Kansas maybe. Look, good job, I know you will have success with him. I gotta run and you need to get to work. Oh, I need you to cover this weekend, about 6 hours both days, bring Steele and Kale with you."

"What's going on, shows."

"No, I'm doing a breed handling clinic in Daytona, or maybe I should say assisting. One of the big time breed handlers. He gets big bucks and a friend of mine got me hooked up to assist. Actually pretty good money for both days.

They finished up the small talk and Kim got in her brand new Ford van and headed back up to New Smyrna. Olivia got ready for work, checked her voice mail, there was no message so she decided she would not return the call when she got home at 6.

Chapter Five

After the New Year 2016 Olivia received two more phone calls with no voice mail message. It was the same number she had received at the agility trial in Orlando in December. She checked out the area code and it matched up to Texas. She didn't know anyone in Texas but her grandfather had lived there for quite a few years prior to his death in 2013. She never visited him there but he occasionally came to Florida and stayed with her and her aunt Kim.

He was in Florida when he died but she was unaware of his visit and as he had stayed in a RV park outside of Tampa. His death was ruled a homicide and was never solved. He was cremated and his remains were sent back to Texas where they were spread by a friend of his who lived in Oklahoma. Olivia and Kim were his only living heirs and he left her a considerable sum of money in trust and a house in rural North Texas. Although Olivia received that lion's share of the estate, Kim was also well compensated. She would occasionally comment that she never figured Rick for one who could handle his money. There were some legal ramifications involved with the will, the trust and the property and the final disposition was delayed several years. Plus the fact that Olivia was still a minor and in her last year of High School when he was murdered. Once the details were ironed out the distribution of the will went forward.

Olivia made numerous attempts to obtain information regarding his murder from the prosecutor's office and the local police who had jurisdiction over his case but never visited in person. She occasionally beat herself up over the fact that her efforts were only e mails and phone calls. After she graduated from High School, found employment and a house to rent she accelerated her efforts to obtain information regarding the case. Her calls and e mails became more persistent but the answers were always the same, no leads and no progress.

The calls from Texas never really stirred any curiosity and she surmised that it was someone who had discovered that she was finally awarded his estate and wanted something from her. She figured that the person was aware of her age and was counting on her naivety to somehow take advantage of her. Sales, opportunities to invest or whatever people tried to do to make money on scams. Internet access to information and public records certainly had her name out there as a potential fish. If it was important the person would have left a voice mail message. She never bothered to try and locate a name though a white pages reverse lookup.

Chapter Six

Olivia's life continued. Juggling her job, training and trialing Steele occasionally and her anemic social life. Olivia rarely dated any longer, not only did she not have the time but her last few tries at a relationship failed miserably. A High School boyfriend dumped her when he went to college on a baseball scholarship. After High School she dated a local contractor, a salesman where she worked and a detective from the Brevard County Prosecutors Office. Nothing clicked and some of the women she knew from her "dog life" made vailed references to her being gay. A few even hit on her and she had to set them straight. She was after all straight, the absence of a boyfriend wasn't any confusion on her part about sexual preference. Even her aunt, who raised her after the death of her mother occasionally questioned her about her sex life.

In July of 2016 she finally answered her cell phone when she recognized the Texas area code.

"Hello, who is this."

"Olivia?"

"I said who is this, you go first." The voice was definitely female.

"My name is Linda Rossi, I know you don't know me and this is all very awkward, but I knew your grandfather and wondered if I could have a few words with you, if this is in fact Olivia Kname."

"Ok, this is Olivia you can go on if you like, I'm not sure what you and I have to discuss but go ahead anyway."

"Olivia, I was in a writing group with your grandfather for about 3 years. We met at a fiction writing class at an extension campus of the University of North Texas."

Olivia interrupted.

"I wasn't aware of any writing or interest that my grandfather had in writing."

"Oh, that's a shame. He was really quite good and wrote some interesting stuff, or works, which is a better way to describe it."

"Ms. Rossi,"

"You can call me Linda."

"Ok, Linda tell me about the group."

"There were five of us, we met about once every three or four weeks, usually at my place, I am centrally located for the group. I live outside of Gainesville, that's where the campus is located. The class was a mix of older people like our group and students who were taking the course as an elective or for remedial work in writing for college. Three women and your grandfather and one other man formed a little group from the class. We still meet but are down to just three people. Before I go any further we were shocked to hear about his death and I should have reached out to you long ago, accept my condolences and apology."

"Ok, not much I can say there, didn't hear much from anyone, I assumed that he had few friends and he never said much about his personal life when he visited with me. He did talk about a friend who lived in Oklahoma, that's about it."

"Any ideas about his death, all we heard was that he was shot, never saw anything on the internet or local papers about him. Oh, other than an obit in a local Whitesboro, Texas paper"

"Is that why you called me Linda, I'm not being smart, just don't understand, after all it has been over three years."

"No, I'm sorry, I'm not trying to pry. The reason is about a book. I was always interested in the Vietnam War, I was about 4 or 5 when it started and 15 when it ended. I grew up in the Philadelphia area and quite a few guys from there lost their lives over there. As a matter of fact a High School in Philadelphia had the most casualties of any school in the country. My next door neighbor's son died there in 1968. He was only 18, I was just a child but I remember him. Kind of a shy kid, not real popular in school, but he always had a smile and a good word for people in the neighborhood. I can still see him, he was on leave before going over, had his uniform on and he looked so proud. He was the only son, his mom and dad never recovered, I think it killed them too. Well anyway I just finished a book called the Mind of an Assassin, written by a John Price, it made the New York Times best sellers list. Well, your grandfather was working on something and he read quite a few passages to our group, well it sounds almost like this book, the Price book. Before you say anything, I finished the book at the end of last year, and went over and over parts of it before I decided to call. Anyway I think you might want to take a look at it, there are parts that I remember that were verbatim, word for word right from Rick, I'm sorry but we all called him Rick, right from his readings."

"Linda, how did you find me, why the effort anyway, what is it to you."

"I looked up the obit, and found your address on the web, I managed to get your number, those things can be found if you use the right tools. I'm sure you understand."

"Yeah I guess, what about the other part, what is it to you."

"Olivia, your grandfather seemed like a really nice guy, he was kind, easy going and a great listener. He always brought food to our meetings, good stuff, not sweets but healthy stuff. I remember him making brisket tacos, homemade, he smoked the brisket himself. Most of all he had a talent and wrote some really great stuff. I just feel that if someone stole his ideas it wouldn't be right."

"Linda, I don't know what to say. Text me the info on the book, and your e mail address, I will read it and get back to you. I never thought he would write, and never about Vietnam. He never talked about it, people say most men that were there never say much about it. Let me look it over, this book, and think this through. This is a lot of stuff to absorb, but thanks, it is good talking to someone who knew my grandfather."

"Olivia, I am relieved, I wasn't sure how you would take this. If you want to talk about Rick, feel free to call me. Occasionally the group would get together and go out and do non-writing stuff, we usually took in at least one or two UNT football games and occasionally met for dinner and drinks. He and I went to a couple of Rangers games, he was a big baseball fan. They were good times, we were five people from different backgrounds and life experiences and I felt that we were more than just a group, that we were actually friends. Good talking to you."

"Thanks Linda, I will be in touch, bye, wait, one more thing, what about the others in the group, did they read this, what do they think."

"That's the hard part, it is kinda hard to share this, since we don't know each other. One person left the group shortly after Rick died, she had some family issues and moved to another state. I tried to reach out to her a few times but she never responded. The other man, Eli, read the book, but never said much, other than he recognized some things from Rick's writing style, things he thought were more than coincidence.

He shied away from my idea of trying to contact you. He and Rick were close in age, Eli is a few years younger than Rick would be. They got along but there was a difference in the way they lived, sort of a long story. Eli is very talented, probably the most talented in the group. Rick recognize that and always encouraged him. But I sensed that Eli was intimidated by Rick's military background. I think he probably avoided service during that period like a lot of guys did, but never discussed the details. I think he was afraid of being judged, but what I knew of your grandfather he would have not judged him. Rick was very low keyed about his service, and never confronted Eli, but I still think Eli was, I don't know put off maybe. The other member, Bobbi, she is a teacher and very liberal. She and Rick got along but often butted heads over political stuff. You know, when we socialized Bobbi might get a few drinks in her and would often make comments about political stuff. A few times she sort of hinted around that Vietnam was a war fought by those who were less smart, I guess that is the best way to put it. She said a few things about atrocities she had read about, it always made me uncomfortable but I actually think your grandfather was amused in a way. He never lost his temper and usually either ignored it or humored her. Anyway, she read the book and refuses to acknowledge any similarities. Sorry, I've run on here and need to let you go, please contact if you need to talk, want to discuss this further. Rick often talked about you, he was a remarkable person. I was very fond of him. Please take care. "

"Linda, I will check the book out but I have nothing to compare it with, as I had no idea of my grandfather's writing. I will call you back, talk to you, bye. Oh, listen thanks for calling, I appreciate the fact that you and my grandfather were friends."

Chapter Seven

William Frederick "Rick" Kname was born on February 21, 1950 in East Greenfield, Ohio. His father, a World War Two veteran, worked as a machinist in a small specialty steel plant and his mother was a homemaker. Rick's sister, Joann, two years his senior was a High School history teacher who had one daughter, Kimberly. Rick struggled in school and by the time he reached High School the only thing that interested him was playing on the school's baseball team. Tall, 6'1" and athletic, the left handed Rick was the best pitcher on the team. He was also one of the best local baseball prospects in the Eastern Ohio and Western Pennsylvania area. But his frustration with and lack of interest in school resulted in him passing on a possible college scholarship for baseball. He convinced his parents to allow him to drop out of school after his junior year and enlist in the US Army in September 1967. With the escalation of the war in Vietnam the Army was eager to take all who wanted to enlist and waived the 18 year old minimum age.

Rick easily adjusted to Army life and was assigned his first tour in Vietnam in March 1968. His MOS was light weapons infantryman and he was assigned to the First Infantry Division, known as the Big Red One. He served two tours in Vietnam and later in his career a tour in Korea.

Rick married his high school girlfriend, Brenda, after his first Vietnam tour. Rick and his wife divorced after 10 years of marriage as the military life put a strain on their relationship.

They had one child, a daughter, Melissa. Rick was not able to maintain a relationship with either his wife or their daughter. To say that Rick and his daughter were estranged is an understatement. Melissa mostly sided with her mom and pretty much shut Rick out. He was transferred often and the marriage was doomed way before they got the divorced.

Melissa had a daughter, Olivia, out of wedlock in 1996. By this time she and her mother had become adversaries. Melissa drifted from relationship to relationship and provided the bare minimum for her daughter. She even came close to losing her to child protective services on two occasions. Not only did she struggle with being a parent but she struggled with an addiction to drugs. Melissa died from a drug overdose in 2003. Brenda had long since moved on, remarried and started a new family. Rick's relationship with his granddaughter was almost non- existent because of the poor relationship between Rick and Melissa. Rather than see her go into the child protective service foster care system Rick's niece, Kimberly Wainwright, obtained custody of her. Kimberly raised Olivia and Rick provided generous financial support and was able to see her from time to time.

Rick was discharged from the Army in 1987, achieving the rank of Sergeant First Class. He took a job with a government contractor, Pacific Engineering, and worked for them as a consultant for 10 years. Pacific Engineering mostly worked on military contracts and Rick spent the better part of the 10 years at various military bases in Texas and Oklahoma. He liked Texas and when he retired from Pacific he settled in North Texas. He obtained a Private Investigators license in Texas and occasionally worked for a small Private Investigation firm based in the Dallas area.

Rick always felt responsible for the premature death of his daughter and blamed himself for their toxic relationship.

Brenda shunned Rick after their divorce and Rick chose not to stay in contact with her. He was afraid of causing problems with her and her new family. Once Olivia and Kimberly adjusted to their relationship Rick was able to take an interest in her life and visited both Olivia and Kim on occasion. Although the visits were sporadic he did manage to establish a positive relationship with his granddaughter.

Chapter Eight

Olivia found the book by John Price in a bookstore at the Merritt Island Mall. The book had already been published in paperback and although not inclined to reading she finished the book in a week. It really meant nothing to her as she had very little knowledge of her grandfather's military career, especially his service in Vietnam. The book did spur a renewed interest in his death and she decided to look a little further into the investigation. Prior to reaching out to the police she exchanged several e mails with Linda Rossi. She explained that the only connection between her grandfather and the author of the book was the information or suspicions stated by Linda.

Detective Billy Woodruff worked for the Dade City Police department and he was the contact person she reached in September 2016. Woodruff agreed to meet with her and discuss the case in person. He re iterated that it was a cold case and the investigation found no leads. It landed on his desk when the original Detective had been promoted to a special state investigative unit. Dade City Police, under an agreement with the Hernando County Prosecutor's Office, had been designated to lead the investigation.

Olivia had second thoughts about this meeting and regretted making the arrangements and the closer the meeting got the more she dreaded the whole idea. Yet something kept telling her to go through with it. She had trouble explaining her relationship with her grandfather to others, it was really hard to say that they were close. His visits were occasional at best and she never went to Texas to visit him. Despite his financial support for her care Olivia learned that he was never really close to his sister or to her aunt, Kim. Kim said that as a child she rarely saw him and believed that her mom and Rick had problems, but she could never figure out exactly what the issues were. The times Olivia had personal contact with him always made her smile. He was easy going, seemed very caring and always took an interest in her activities. Despite his background she often pictured a gentle and somewhat sensitive man, not a career soldier who had served multiple tours in Vietnam. When the day approached she drove to Dade City and to meet with Detective Woodward.

Chapter Nine

September 1970, Sergeant Rick Knapp, Specialist 4th Class Franklin "Eddie" Spader, and Specialist 4th Class Clifford Nauvana moved towards a prearranged rendezvous with a mechanized infantry unit attached to the 25th Infantry Division. They had left a hamlet, or sub division of a village about 10 Kilometers from the Cambodian border. It was about 2PM, 1400 hours in military time. Typical Vietnam weather, hot and humid with occasional passing clouds which gave some relief from the heat. They tried to stay off the main trails as no doubt the VC traveled the same ones and probably booby trapped some. The terrain was partially covered but intermittently opened up to fields and rice paddies.

They walked in single file and the closer they got to the pre-arranged point, the easier the terrain became. The trails near the village of Duc Hue took them through paddy lands, past a long canal and through an area of clustered hamlets intersecting trails leading to the road.

Rick, on his second tour in Vietnam, walked in the lead and they spaced themselves about 20 meters apart. The area had been relatively quiet in the past few weeks. Intelligence had indicated that the Viet Cong units operating in the area had crossed over into Cambodia to resupply and rest. Their mission had nothing to do with recon but what command called an intervention. Command was vague regarding the nature of the intervention. It was clear that the American and South Vietnam Armies wanted what was called "white hamlets." In other words no Viet Cong presence. That fact was more or less the object of the mission. The communists had other ideas. When they passed near hamlets they noted only women, children and elderly men. If the VC weren't in Cambodia they were hiding out in one of the many tunnel complexes.

Rick carried an Ithaca 12 gauge model 37 shotgun. A modified version of the weapon for military use in Vietnam. He preferred it over standard issue M-16 assault rifle used by the American forces in Vietnam. He also carried a Smith and Wesson 38 caliber revolver in a holster attached to his web gear. Again he opted for this model over the standard issue 45 caliber Colt 1911 semi-automatic pistol issued to the Army and Marines. The Smith was issued to pilots in the Air Force and Navy but Rick managed to requisition one for his own use. It required a trade for an AK-47 assault rifle that Rick had taken from a dead Viet Cong soldier on his first tour in Vietnam.

His tall and lean body gave the appearance of his fatigues hanging on him, rather than fitting him. He wore a boonie hat rather than a steel pot and had cut the sleeves off of his fatigue shirt rather than roll them up, this drew frowns from command staff when they were in base camp.

Next in line was Clifford Nauvana, slightly built and dark complexed, he was only 18 years old. Cliff carried an M-16 and humped the PRC 25 radio along with his ammunition and web gear. Cliff wore an Army issue baseball cap and unauthorized sunglasses purchased from the Vietnamese civilians in one of the villages. Cliff had enlisted in the Army right out of High school rather than being drafted. Clifford stood about 5'8" tall and probably weighed about 130 lbs. He was quiet but very cool under pressure. One of the reasons he had been chosen for this "unit." That is if you could call three men a unit.

Keeping up the rear was Franklin "Eddie" Spader, also on his second tour in Vietnam. Eddie, as he preferred to be called, beguiled his awkward body type. What appeared to be a slightly overweight and clumsy frame was actually coordinated, deceptively fast and strong as an ox. He was about 5'10" tall and probably carried an extra 15 or 20 pounds. Even in this climate he was unable to get his weight down. He moved with an uncanny grace through the terrain. Eddie carried an M-16 rifle and the standard issue 45 caliber handgun in a shoulder holster. A Colt model 1911 to be exact. This one was chrome plated with pearl handles. The serial number had been filed off and Eddie was not very specific as to where or how he had obtained the weapon. Eddie wrapped a camouflage bandana around his forehead and had a boonie hat tucked into one of the side pockets of his jungle fatigue pants. All three packed very little in the way of provisions as they had been dropped off just before dawn and the scheduled pick up was for early afternoon. As they neared the pickup point Rick signaled back to Clifford and Eddie that he could hear the mechanized infantry unit the distance.

They met the column of Armored Personnel Carriers and infantrymen on foot at the intersection of two dirt roads. The unit looked haggard as they had been working search and seal operations non- stop for 30 days. Mostly young draftees with that look of exhaustion on their faces. They were on their way to a night defensive position where Rick and his two man unit would be picked up by helicopter and taken back to base camp. The officer in charge, a Lieutenant who looked to be all of 20 years old stopped the column and had a brief conversation with Rick. Pickings were slim for soldiers in this unpopular war as were the selection of officers and NCO's.

Rumor was that they would take about anyone in OCS. The graduation percentage was unusually high. Rick sized the LT up and noted that he seemed to have a pretty good hold on things. The young draftees listened to him and he approached them with a level of respect necessary for a leader and they seemed to hold the same respect for him. Rick figured he was probably one of the good ones.

Eddie immediately started banter with a few of the unit grunts, his favorite past time when not on a mission. He lit a cigarette took a long drink from one of his canteens and started as they say smoking and joking with several of the grunts. Once everything was in order the LT told the column to move out. He let Rick know that the area designated for the night defensive position was only about 1 Kilometer away. They were ahead of schedule.

Rick and Eddie opted to walk along adjacent to the PC's, while Clifford climbed up on the second PC in line. He shed the heavy radio and loosened his web gear. Rick called up to Cliff, "Cliff call Stantone and tell him the trifecta cashed in, will give him details when we get back to base camp."

Cliff smiled, " keep it simple right Sarge."

"Yeah man, no details over the airwaves, he can wait, I got to think about how I want to write the report anyway, and what he is looking for you and Eddie didn't see anyhow."

Eddie chimed in, "hey how in the fuck did Stantone end up over here anyway, you know I hear his family is deep in money."

Eddie left it there and went back to talking to the grunts. They were discussing R and R's and who got the most pussy. Hong Kong seemed to be the favorite and several compared notes with Eddie on the bars and the whores. Eddie was well versed, as he had two R and R's already but he was on his second tour. He figured he would get at least one more. He told them he was trying to get another but maybe Bangkok this time.

Stantone was Captain Ron Stantone the officer in charge of their detail. Stantone's family owned racehorses and he was involved in the family business. When they had to make a code name for a mission he used horse racing terms. Probably as good a cover as any, it seemed highly unlikely that anyone listening in would be able to match the terms with the military objective. Rick figured that Stantone's family was connected enough where he could have avoided military service but he was here anyway. Stantone never provided details and Rick never asked.

Rick called back up to Clifford, "anything back from Stantone that I should know about right now. We will probably be back there before dusk, depends on how quick the chopper gets us out of the NDP."

Clifford yelled back over the sound of the Armored Personnel Carriers, referred to as APC's by the grunts, grinding along the road. "he said he can't wait, but you know him, trying to be funny."

Chapter Eleven

Early October and the Florida weather was perfect, sunny, warm and not too humid. John Price walked out to the deck attached to his two bedroom home on the scenic Banana River. He had recently purchased the home with proceeds from his successful novel and was finally living the dream. The house was a bargain but needed work as the previous owners had allowed it to become a little run down. In their haste to get divorced they allowed him to offer way less than market value. It was livable and he had already discussed improvements with a contractor and work was to start early in 2017.

John's agent encouraged him to get working on something new, the old "strike when the iron is hot" theory. John wasn't currently motivated and he was enjoying his notoriety. He had recently been invited to speak to a fiction writing class at a satellite campus of the University of Central Florida in Daytona Beach. They were even going to pay him.

John didn't know Rick Kname. He had read his obituary after the manuscript was submitted for publishing. He had forgotten that the only relatives of Kname lived within 50 miles of his present home. He didn't lose any sleep over it. Few had questioned the topic of his book or where he had obtained the idea. When asked questions regarding research he winged it at first and later goggled topics about the Vietnam War. He learned his lesson at some early book signings and wanted to make sure he wasn't put in an awkward position again. He even read two historical novels about the war and knew more than enough to field and successfully answer questions. As far as he knew the actual document he plagiarized wasn't previously circulated and was unaware that anyone had accessed the laptop prior to him purchasing it from the flea market vendor. He never liked the term plagiarized, and in his mind he substituted it for borrowed. He figured that if he changed certain parts, even slightly, he could avoid anyone questioning the originality of his work.

John even researched Kname to determine if he had anything published under his name or another name. He came up blank and figured that the writing in the laptop was something he had not finished or perfected and died before submitting the manuscript to anyone. He realized that maybe this was just a stroke of luck. He wondered if the content had anything to do with Kname's demise. He hoped not, but nothing unusual in the way of threats had come his way. He was always able to put these thoughts out of his mind. He figured it wasn't worth the worry.

John leaned back on his recliner adjusted the position and admired the view he had from the deck of his new home. He smiled to himself and tried to imagine what it would look like once a few upgrades had been completed. He opened a bottle of Corona, lit a cigarette and watched the rich people cruise by in their boats on the Banana River.

Chapter Twelve

Olivia drove from Mims to Dade City to meet with Detective Billy Woodruff early one morning in October, 2016. It is about a two hour drive. She mapped it on her lap top and took what she called the scenic route. Back roads through rural Central Florida on a sunny and warm October morning. She stopped in Eustis and had a quick breakfast at a pancake house. She sat at the counter and the waitress, a 40 something women with tattoos on both forearms and purple highlights in her hair, waited on her. She used the time worn vocabulary in addressing Olivia such as hon and dear. She made Olivia uncomfortable as she seemed to stare at her in an unnatural way. Olivia played it off as she was somewhat nervous about the meeting with Woodruff. She felt as if she were over reacting. Anyway she ordered coffee and a short stack of pancakes. Left a three dollar tip and hurried back to her car and continued the drive to Dade City.

When she arrived at the police headquarters she was about 20 minutes ahead of the prearranged meeting time. She waited in the lobby until Woodruff came out and asked her to come back to the detective section. They met in an office, she wasn't sure if it was shared with another detective or not. There was no sign on the door.

She guessed him to be in his early 40's. Balding and a little on the heavy side but sort of handsome in an odd way. There were no family pictures in his office but a diploma from the University of Florida hung on the wall. His tie was already pulled loose from his light blue oxford dress shirt and he removed a light weight navy blue sport coat and hung it on a hook by the doorway. She noticed a handgun holstered on his right hip. He smiled and looked her up and down. She got the impression he liked her look but in a not creepy way.

"Hi Olivia, I'm Billy Woodruff, how was your trip over from the other coast."

"Good, nice meeting you." Olivia decided that she would dress up a little, her job only required casual dress. She wore a little makeup, out of character for her, and a light grey sleeveless dress with the hem just above her knees. She had let her hair grow out a little, and had it pulled back in a short pony tail.

"Have a seat, from our phone conversation and e mail exchanges I know that you have a copy of the police, crime report. I'm not sure how or where I can help you." Woodruff seemed at ease but she could tell there was some information not in the report and she hoped he was going to disclose it to her.

"Detective,"

"Olivia, not formal here, you can call me Billy."

"What can you tell me that isn't in the report."

"You went right to the juggler. Really nothing. Sammons was the lead, he wasn't able to make any progress on this and now I have an almost three year old murder investigation on my hands."

Olivia leaned back, "isn't it your job, did you know Sammons, did he ever I don't know take a guess, have any ideas not in the report. You mentioned in your e mails that it was a cold case."

Woodruff was a little put back, Olivia had gone straight to the point and was somewhat aggressive.

"That's a lot of questions at once, do you always talk so fast."

Woodruff didn't give her a chance to answer, now it had quickly become a contest of sorts, right off the bat.

"That's the problem, Sammons wasn't a very good detective, nice guy just not a good cop. His uncle is politically connected and got him the job and then got him moved up to a cushy State Investigation Unit job. Quite frankly he was intimidated by a murder investigation."

Olivia shot back, "that's it, I drove all this way and like couldn't you tell me this over the phone, should I be talking to him, Sammons or whatever his name is."

"Sammons would find a way not to talk to you. I'm not undermining him here, everyone around here knew how he was. He just wasn't a very good investigator. He was what you call book smart. Could wow you with his knowledge of policy and procedure. Always received high marks when he went to trainings. Just couldn't convert it to the job, he wasn't what they call street smart. Now he pushes papers in Tallahassee with some special unit, probably never has to go into the field, probably never has to knock on doors."

Woodruff continued.

"Olivia, I wasn't comfortable discussing this on the phone or over e mails. I mean how would I even know it was really you. There is a story, but I had to ask someone higher up first before relating it."

"OK Billy this better be good."

"First, are you going out on your own with this, how come now after almost 3 years?"

Olivia was a little offended over the comment.

"I was only 17, I was still in High School when my grandfather was killed. There was a lot of legal stuff, he had a will but the executor was someone I didn't know, there were issues with the title to his house, I could go on and on. Anyway what do you mean by am I going out on my own over this."

Woodruff smartly side stepped that comment, he realized his choice of words was poor and out of line.

"I think you are referring to Franklin Spader, the executor, he lives in Oklahoma. I think they call him Eddie."

"Yeah, do you know him."

"Yeah, we talked on the phone a few times, I actually met him. He came out here to handle the property. He took possession of the firearms and personal items found in the RV and took care of all the matters regarding the RV. I think he got it sold, I guess you know all that, since you said you talked to the lawyer. Everything was handled through the lawyer from Dallas, all above board, I'm sure you are aware of that."

"Hey I never said I spoke to the lawyer, but yeah, I spoke to him a few times, but never spoke to Spader. I reached out to him but have been unsuccessful in reaching him, I guess I'm not in his loop."

"Are you suspicious of him, like maybe he was holding back."

Olivia laughed, "What are you trying to do here, throw him under the bus like, whatever that detective's name is, Sammons right."

Again Woodruff deflected, he was sure at this point Olivia was looking for an argument, he kind of liked her spunk, considered that she might be a good detective herself.

"Listen, Spader is smart, he must have been trusted by your grandfather and far as I could gather had nothing to gain, they must have been good friends."

"Billy, did you talk with him about the murder, did anyone?"

"Ok Olivia, let me tell you the story. We have been shorthanded for officers for years. And getting good officers, that's another conversation. The current administration in Washington has fostered a hatred and distrust of law enforcement nationwide, but I'll pass on that discussion. The sheriff's deputy who responded to the original 911 call was just out of training and on his first shift by himself. It was about an hour before shift change and the call was originally interpreted by dispatch as a non- emergency. Typical late night, early morning BS call. Or at least that is what the dispatcher thought. We had been getting a lot of nuisance calls from that park, it was a request to look at a suspicious situation. People often use that term when they can't think of anything else or have nothing really to report. I guess whoever killed your grandfather left the door to the RV ajar and it eventually came open. The caller said that he suspected something "amiss" but nothing more. The dispatcher takes the call and sends the new officer out, figuring it is just what I said, a BS call. Like I said he is brand new, actually not even fully trained. We were taking any recruits we could attract early from the training academy, allowing them to complete the training after a few months on the job. On the job training, in law enforcement not a good policy, but as they say it is what it is. Unfortunately he walks in and finds a murder scene. He actually compromised the murder scene, not on purpose but just from lack of experience."

"None of this was in the report, right."

"Yeah, actually someone else wrote his report since he was new, it was the next deputy coming on. Long story short, and this is already a long story, his name is Jim Vanderkelen, he is currently retired but it is he you probably need to talk to."

Olivia shook her head as Woodruff paused, took a deep breath and continued.

"Vanderkelen wasn't always a sheriff's deputy. He was a major crimes detective with Tampa PD, and a damn good one. Long story short, again, he made a mistake and ended up in a world of crap. His section chief hated him and tried to get him fired, like only 4 or 5 years before he was eligible for pension. Anyway the union made a deal, and he took a reassignment and demotion and ended up here. The chief here at the time was a good friend of one of the deputy chiefs at Tampa PD and made sure that Jim got dumped on while he put the time in to get his pension. Jim worked hard and always did his job. He documented the crime scene that morning and actually filed the report. He was careful not to allow the rookie to start out his career behind the eight ball. After that he took an interest in the case and tried to help Sammons out, I'm sure he also gave him some advice but Sammons probably just ignored it. Sammons was like everybody else, he knew Jim's history and didn't want anyone thinking he was on Jim's side. Even though Jim knew what everybody else knew, that this was a hit, he probably has more knowledge of this case than anyone. Jim also forgot more about detective work than most the others ever knew. Certainly more than Sammons. After all, no brainer, who takes someone's life, leaves no evidence and takes nothing from the premises. There was over 700 in cash in the night stand, not to mention a pistol, a shotgun a laptop and on and on."

Olivia thought for a second, "I never saw anything about an interview with the person who made the call in the report you sent me, I hope that was accomplished, he was interviewed, right."

"Yeah, but he is what you would call a wise guy. Vacations down here for three or four months a year, lives in a cold state, Michigan or Wisconsin, I think. Family owns a business, trucking company. He also has a record, petty stuff, whatever.

He refused to say anything more than he woke up to take a piss and looked outside and saw the door open, his RV was about three lots from your grandfather's. Threatened to lawyer up, can you imagine, just over that. Vanderkelen said he watches too much crime stuff on TV. "

"So what now, do you think this Vanderkelen guy will talk to me."

"I already spoke to him when I knew you were coming over. He lives in Trilby, not far from here. Right now he holds a PI license and takes just easy surveillance stuff, you know divorce evidence stuff, insurance fraud stuff like that. Here is his card. Call him."

"What did he do, why was he demoted."

"Google it, there are articles in the Tampa paper, happened about 8 to 10 years ago. I don't want to, you know get into it, ask him. Who knows, he might even tell you."

"How well did you know him."

"I worked at the County as an investigator before I took the detective job here, but I was here a few years before he retired. I liked him, he got a bad deal, thrown under the bus as you would say, but he never allowed it to compromise his work ethic. You gotta respect that."

Woodruff reached across his desk with a manila folder and handed it to Olivia.

"I got permission to give you this, Vanderkelen's deputy report, the complete official report and the inventory sheet from the evidence locker. If you look you will see that when we turned the personal stuff over to Spader, the laptop was missing. Before you yell, if it had been the cash, or the guns they would have turned this place upside down to find out who took it. It's just that so many people have access, detectives, deputies, county investigators, prosecutors, you name it, it would be like finding a needle in a haystack. Also it took Spader about almost two years to get the stuff, you know, legal stuff, clearances whatever. The guns were sent to a Federal Firearms licensed dealer in Oklahoma by Spader. He didn't want the hassle of claiming the guns at the airport to satisfy the airline and the federal statutes for transporting firearms. All the paperwork, he called it crap he didn't need to be bothered with. Everything else he took."

"When you met him did he say anything about the missing laptop. Maybe the laptop had information about why my grandfather was killed."

Woodruff laughed, "yeah, Spader, he flew in here from Dallas. He went over everything and he questioned the laptop. Made us write a letter to the lawyer in Dallas confirming it was missing from evidence. He took a copy. Wasn't going to leave himself out there, to be blamed. Quite the character. If it contained anything, whoever took it probably deleted everything on the laptop."

Olivia asked, "do you think Vanderkelen ever talked to him?"

"Ask him, by the looks of Spader he and Jimmy could have been drinking buddies."

Olivia shrugged her shoulders, she realized that Woodruff wasn't going to say anything else. Olivia and Woodruff exchanged goodbyes and Olivia left and headed back to Brevard County.

Chapter Thirteen

Franklin Edward Spader was born in 1950. His mother and father never married but lived together until Franklin's father died in 1970. They lived in south - central Oklahoma near the Texas border. His mom, Janet, worked at various restaurants as a waitress and his dad, Edward, was a ranch hand at local cattle and horse ranches. They never had much but did a relatively good job of raising Franklin and provided more than just the basics. Franklin had a happy childhood and often went with his father to the various ranches where he worked. He used to always say that Eddie could ride a horse before he could walk. An exaggeration for sure, but the sequence wasn't far off. He never liked being called Frank or Franklin and preferred to be called Eddie. Franklin was the name of his paternal grandfather, who had passed away before Eddie was born.

Eddie was a restless child who never did well in school and preferred the outdoors, hunting, fishing and as he got older working with his father on the ranches. In 1967 he talked his parents into signing him out of school and he joined the US Army just after turning 17. Like many others early enlistments were taken as it became apparent that the Vietnam War was going to put a strain on the draft and deter young men from enlisting. It was also common place for parents to support their boys by helping them lie about their age when necessary for acceptance into the military. Most recruiters were willing to turn their heads the other way.

Despite his lack of education he did well on the Army intelligence tests and ended up with a support Military Occupational Specialty (MOS). Even when he was in school his lack of interest never overshadowed the fact that he was smart and picked things up easily. He was assigned to an Army supply unit when he was shipped to Vietnam in late 1967. When he arrived he was sent to a MACV (Military Assistance Command Vietnam) compound near Saigon. He was promoted to specialist 4th class after about 6 months and more or less ran the unit. The NCO in charge of the supply unit was biding his time getting ready to DEROS (Destination Estimate Return Over Seas) and would have only one year left until retirement. The NCO spent most of his time at the base camp NCO club chasing the young Vietnamese women who worked at the club. Spader did his job, and the NCO's job and never complained. Right before the NCO got his orders to go back home he and Spader got into an argument and Spader was written up, given an Article 15 and busted back to PFC.

After the NCO left his replacement was a clueless lifer just as bad as his predecessor. He also spent most of his time drinking in the NCO club, telling war stories from his first tour in 1965 and Spader continued to run the unit. The result was a smooth functioning operation that kept the line units well supplied. Spader often volunteered to accompany resupply convoys to various base camps in the Three Corps war zone. Eventually, right before Spader returned from Vietnam, he was promoted back to specialist 4th class.

Spader was reassigned to Ft. Sill, Oklahoma and this made him happy. He could visit family and he was able to spend some time with his father who was in failing health. Oklahoma was in his blood, but he soon became restless and re-enlisted for three more years and volunteered to go back to Vietnam. He got his wish in late 1969.

This time he was assigned to Cu Chi and the 25th Infantry Division. The commanding officer of the 25th Admin Company took a liking to Spader and assigned him as his personal driver. Eddie came to know an infantry platoon sergeant by the name of Rick Kname. Kname's unit was back in the base camp from time to time and Rick talked to Spader about a special unit that he was going to be in charge of. Spader was curious but Kname was keeping the details to himself, as he said "until everything was set in stone." Spader questioned him as to why he would want someone in the field with no combat experience. Kname told him that the desire was the most important thing and he had observed that Spader was independent and able to take responsibility when needed. Spader agreed, and a bond ensued but also a friendship that would change Eddie in more ways than one. Rick and Eddie remained friends until Rick's death in 2013.

After he returned from his second tour in Vietnam Spader re-enlisted one more time. He had various duty stations but never again got his primary choice, Ft. Sill. He longed for Oklahoma and wanted to be near his family. He missed his father and regretted not being able to spend more time with him prior to his death in 1970. After 9 ½ years in the Army Spader passed on another re- enlistment and he returned to Oklahoma and made it his home. He got a job working for the State of Oklahoma in various departments ending his career working for the department of workers compensation. He had a good mind for managing money and he purchased a home near Durand in south central Oklahoma near the Texas border. He retired from the State in 2002 and went back to working part time as a ranch hand, much like his father. He was financially set enough where he could work only when he pleased and only for who he pleased.

Chapter Fourteen

Olivia drove back to Brevard County and could not get the meeting out of her mind. She wondered if contacting Vanderkelen would be worth the effort but decided to skip contacting him for the time being. She was disappointed at the meeting with Woodruff and besides having the deputy's report and the list of belongings taken from the RV she learned nothing more. It seemed as though it was a write off, a professional hit with no leads or no clues. She always wondered what her grandfather could have been into to make him the target of a hit man. She also worried about the opinion of others, as to why did it take her almost three years to become interested in the case. She always failed to consider the fact that when he was killed she was still in High School. The crack by Woodruff about her waiting bothered her but she realized she had to separate herself from the guilt.

When she returned home her focus went back to her job, helping out her aunt and Steele. He was again invited to the Invitational in Orlando in December and she resumed training him for the event. She had also started training JD, her new rescue project taken on after her pit bull Kale had died, in agility foundation classes. Running her dogs gave her a purpose and it helped her pass the time in what she often described in her thoughts as a dull life. Kim was pretty easy on her and asked for minimal commitment helping out at the boarding facility. Sometimes she thought that her aunt asked for the help because she wanted the company. The world of showing dogs in confirmation was pretty cutthroat and Kim had made a lot of enemies. In dogs that usually meant you were good, and Kim was good. She had a soft touch and could move a dog around the ring with grace and confidence.

Her job was also easy and she was required to only work no more than 30 hours per week. Her employer wanted to avoid having to pay her benefits, and usually she got at least 25 hours, which was fine with her. There were some perks. She got discount prices on service for her SUV and her hours were flexible. She never had to work nights and had almost all Saturday's off. The dealership was closed on Sunday's so that was never an issue. If she had to miss a few days there was no push back from her boss.

Olivia finally got around to searching Jim Vanderkelen on the internet. There were numerous articles written regarding his situation at the Tampa PD. There was even an interesting editorial in the Tampa Tribune.

Vanderkelen and his partner Detective Ross Burns were investigating a case in one of the local High Schools. A teacher was having sexual contact with two students and although the affairs were consensual, one of the girls was under the age of consent when the affairs started. The girls never disclosed, but the younger one bragged to a friend about "fucking a football coach" and the rumor eventually got to the principal. Normally this would be a case solely for the Department of Children and Families, but the fact that the one girl was under 16 raised it to the level where the allegations prompted criminal charges.

At some point during the investigation Vanderkelen started seeing one of the teachers, a physical education teacher who also coached one of the girls in field hockey. Vanderkelen knew better and was married at the time. The teacher, 10 years his junior, was also aware that he was married but got involved with him despite the circumstances. The teacher, Allison March, was considered a possible witness because of her player coach relationship to the girl. Allison was also a co-worker of the alleged perpetrator, who not only taught at the school but was an assistant football coach. Vanderkelen and March's indiscretions got them into a world of shit.

Vanderkelen and March kept the affair low key but Burns suspected the arrangement and confronted Vanderkelen. Vanderkelen figured that Burns wasn't bluffing and he just told the truth. Unfortunately Burns and Vanderkelen had a poor working relationship and Burns took the opportunity to damage his partner's clean record and reputation. Burns was always on the defensive and tired of the fact that Vanderkelen was a much better investigator than he. Burns went to the section chief, who always hated Vanderkelen, and eventually he was demoted and had to take a deputy sheriff's job in Dade City to save his pension.

Olivia was able to piece the scenario together based on the newspaper articles regarding the case and she was able to put two and two together and see how Vanderkelen was demoted and transferred. The editorial was the most telling and the journalist used the case to lead into further editorials on patronage in the department. He referred to the actions taken against Vanderkelen as an attempt to hide other, more serious discretions in the department and painted Vanderkelen as a scapegoat who at most should have been suspended for a period of time and moved to another department at Tampa PD.

Olivia decided to at least give it a shot and see what he had to offer. It was on her to do list after the Invitational in December.

Chapter Fifteen

Slider possessed various identities but his real name was Thomas Crowe. He was born in Union City, New Jersey in 1972. His mother was a 17 year old "flower child," or hippie. His father was a drummer in a traveling cover bar band and never had any input into Thomas' life. He probably didn't even know he was the father. His mother's input was also limited as Thomas was placed in foster care at age 3 ½ due to mom's heroin addiction. Her addiction would eventually kill her at the tender age of 22.

Thomas spent most of his childhood and all of his adolescence in the New Jersey foster care and residential facility system. He was briefly adopted at age 5, but for all practical purposes was "given back" like damaged goods by age 7. The social workers who represented the child protective services system blamed the failed adoption a result of Thomas' lack of socialization. There were however several referrals on the family for both abuse and neglect issues. The agency investigated and the record reflected that all but one were unfounded. One investigation had a finding of unsubstantiated with concerns. The concerns cited in the record were vague and Thomas remained in the home until the couple signed surrenders and sent him back to the system. The young couple were prime for another attempt so they skated from any criticism or fault. The agency had more failed adoptions than it cared to admit to.

The residential facilities were a lesson in survival. Institutionalized adolescents learn real life skills, such as lying and manipulating staff and case managers. The case managers are saddled with way too many cases making it virtually impossible to keep abreast of the child's progress and safety. Some of the agencies that the system contracts to assist in the care and supervision of the children take way more money from the state than the services rendered merit. The state touts the system as successful but from the child's view the system sucks. Most come out bitter but tough and worldly beyond their years. Thomas had no family supports what so ever so planning beyond the age of 18 was a crap shoot.

One positive for Thomas was that his last two years in the system were in a residential facility in Somerset County. Some of the residents were allowed to attend school in the local school district. The district was in an affluent area made up of mostly upper middle class families. Most of the facility residents attending the schools in the district stuck out like a sore thumb. Thomas had just passing grades and his behavior was just on the right side of acceptable, allowing him to remain in the school. He was athletic, wiry and strong for his size. He got permission from the staff at the residential facility to try out for the High School wrestling team. He made the squad and lost only 4 matches in two years. Twice he went to the regional finals in his weight class and once got to the state tournament where he finished 3rd in his class. His coach was a big part of his success. He encouraged Thomas to toe the line and stay in the school as the alternative would have been attending school at the facility, there he could not participate in sports at the school.

After he graduated from High School and aged out of the system at 18 his coach encouraged him to join the military. Because Thomas was a ward of the state, meaning that the state had guardianship of him, he was left with few choices upon reaching the age of 18. Thomas had no family and the system had no provisions for helping him after his 18th birthday. He was as they say "on his own."   Right after graduation he joined the US Navy. As it out turned out the wrestling coach was one of the few adults in Thomas' life that took more than a casual interest in him.

Thomas was stationed for most of his four year enlistment at the Naval Air base in San Diego. Thomas had a good mechanical aptitude and he was trained as a mechanic on military aircraft. He really didn't like the Navy and he didn't like his job but he maintained a clean record. After his four year enlistment he was honorably discharged with no violations under the Uniform Code of Military Justice. Thomas' future employer preferred candidates with military backgrounds and usually opted for those who had under the radar jobs. The military taught discipline and the employer knew that was a key to success in the job. They also believed that you didn't need to be in special ops or a Marine Corps sniper to have the profile they were looking for. Candidates with good eye sight and better than average hand eye coordination could be taught the skills needed for the job. A bitterness towards society was also a plus.

After his discharge he lived in the San Diego area and worked as a civilian employee at the Naval Base doing basically the same job he did in the Navy. He met a women that also worked for the Navy as a civilian and they became romantically involved. They shared an apartment and this would turn out to be the first serious relationship in Thomas' life. Most of his relationships while in the Navy were one night stands. Obviously growing up in the system he was never able to develop the type of skills needed to have a successful relationship as an adult. When adolescents went beyond casual relationships in facilities it was always on the sly. Being caught in a sexual tryst meant being put on punishment. Because the facilities had to segregate males from females sometimes the sexual contact was of the same sex type. Thomas had no interest in having sex with another male, therefore he came out of the system with limited social skills and little sexual experience with females.

Thomas became bored with the job and had issues maintaining honesty and trust with his girlfriend. He was unable to share and reluctant to express any feelings towards her. She tried to cope and made an honest effort to give their arrangement a chance. It was hard for her to break his shell and even harder for her to understand why he was the way he was. Eventually she moved out, frustrated because she had feelings for him but just never thought it would work. Had it not been for an ad in the local newspaper for an employment opportunity Thomas, or as he would later be known as Slider, might have just continued working for the Navy and living in the San Diego area.

Chapter Sixteen

The ad asked those who wanted a fast paced profession that required travel to apply within. The ad was posted in the jobs section of a local advertisement publication distributed in the area. A free paper that was left in most local businesses, such as laundromats, car repair shops, public transportation waiting areas and bars and restaurants. The Parallax Group sought prospects in the San Diego area and promised lucrative jobs for those who qualified. The ad provided very little regarding details about the positions. It listed an 800 number and requested interested parties to call and leave a message as to how the interested party could be reached. Thomas decided to call. He left his phone number at the apartment and waited.

The Parallax Group was actually just one person. He was a "finder" for several corporations, some of whom accepted government work on a contract basis. Most of the firms were not household names and several only existed on paper. It took a week but the finder reached Thomas and made an appointment for them to meet. He deferred giving details about the job citing that it was better to discuss these things in person. The address was just outside San Diego in a small strip mall with six store fronts, mostly of the service type businesses such as nail salons, tattoo parlors and small fast food places.

The storefront was Spartan looking inside and out. The office was small with cheap furniture that looked like it had been recycled from businesses with very low budgets. Thomas dressed in a jacket, tie and neatly pressed chinos for the interview. The interviewer only identified himself as Mr. Sparks. Sparks was short, bald, overweight and dressed in a golf shirt, and cheap polyester pants that were a little too tight. When he stood up to shake hands he seemed kind of bent over, like he couldn't stand up straight. His handshake was of the dead fish variety.

The conversation was odd to say the least. Sparks asked questions about previous employment, inquired about any criminal history and asked for a description of family background. When Thomas relayed his past, from the fact that he had no family, grew up in the system to being honorably discharged from the Navy, Sparks became very interested. It was almost as if Thomas was trying to discourage any further contact but the bleak description of his background seemed to peak the interested Sparks had in him.

Thomas inquired about the job, what were the duties, how much travel, pay scale, medical insurance, opportunities for promotion and so on and so forth. Just the usual questions one would ask. Sparks was very vague, to the point that Thomas wanted to walk out but for some reason he stayed. Sparks said that before the details could be disclosed he would have to take a battery of tests. Sparks referred to the job as "having very special qualities not present in most individuals." Sparks was skilled at baiting the hook and he managed to get Thomas to agree to being tested. Thomas filled out a very generic application and Sparks told him they would be in touch. It was obvious that the employer wanted to do some background checks prior to testing.

Chapter Seventeen

It was a few weeks before Sparks called Thomas back and he informed him that the testing process would take a few weeks. The first session consisted of a written battery of test that reminded Thomas of the initial testing he took to join the Navy. It looked like basic aptitude multiple choice questions. He had no idea of whether he was doing well or not and some of the questions seemed odd in nature to him. It almost appeared as though they were screening for people with "bad attitudes." The test administrator was Sparks and they met in the same office front where he had the initial interview. Sparks sat in the same room reading the newspaper and at times it looked like he was falling asleep. After about three hours of testing Sparks told him that after this group, which is how he referred to the tests, were evaluated they may ask him back for the advanced session.

Thomas figured he would never hear from them again but he got another call within one week. Again he met Sparks at the store front, which appeared as though it hadn't been used for anything since the last session. Even the same edition of the newspaper Sparks was reading was still on the table. This time there was a monitor set up and Sparks said that he would have to view the slide show and answer each question quickly. Thomas had a small hand held device with three keys, yes, no, not sure. Sparks started the slide show and within 30 minutes the test was over. The questions were odd, and again Thomas felt as though they were looking for people with attitude issues caused by abuse and abandonment backgrounds. Two examples of questions that really stuck out in his mind were, "I really got a raw deal out of life," "I never knew my father" and "I have extensive experience using firearms." Sparks told him that he would let him know one way or another within a week, but advised him if chosen be prepared to start "almost immediately."

Thomas started his career for the employer in the early spring of 1998. The company took care of all of his needs. His job was to kill people. Simple as that. No such thing as a training program, it was seat of the pants on the job training. They were a well- oiled machine. Everything was provided, identifications, weapons, credit cards, cash and lodging when on assignment. He never saw a credit card bill, obviously someone was paying the expenses. He never paid rent, or charges for leasing a vehicle. He never used the same gun twice, they were picked up and dropped off as per instructions. Sometimes they were dropped off at a gun dealer, and there were situations where he felt that they knew who he was as soon as he entered the store. He also always carried a personal handgun, documentation and permits were always provided. He carried but knew that he was never to use his personal piece on a job.

Thomas was blessed with a good memory and he never had problems with the details of his phony ID's or the background or pertinent information on his hits. He was required to change his residence from time to time. He never owned anything because accumulating personal belongings could lead to being discovered. Everything in his apartments was leased under the name of various shell companies. If he had to change locations quickly he had nothing to leave behind. He usually opted for warmer climates near the water, a habit obtained from being stationed and living in the San Diego area. Sometimes he went for months without an assignment and sometimes he was killing every few weeks. Most of his hits were actually easy. Sometimes it seemed too easy. He often wondered who was killing all these people but realized early on that it didn't make sense to wonder why. Must be a lot of money floating around because sometimes he was paid very well for his jobs and there was never any delay in payment. The "fees" were always direct deposited into one of his various accounts, all of course under different names. Although he rarely tried to figure out why his target was being hit, he occasionally saw where one of his hits made a local newspaper and then as the technology developed the internet. Everything was ordered and discussed in code, even his name, Slider, was code.

It was late 2016 and he had just finished a particularly hard assignment. The presidential campaign and election of 2016 had been a bitter fight and had divided the country. That coupled with the divide caused by the previous administration led to a toxic atmosphere. The hatred escalated even before the president elect was sworn in. Slider figured that this hit had been ordered because of political reasons and the animosity between the two political parties.

The "company" had directed him to hit a man who lived in the Seattle area. This was an area he hated mostly for the weather and partly because a once beautiful city had been overrun with homelessness and drug issues. After completing the hit he read on the internet about murder and it stated that the victim was killed in a gay bar in a suburb of Seattle. He also located some information regarding a conspiracy theory about the murder. It stated that the victim was about to go public with damaging personal information on a long time liberal member of the US Senate. The Senator was a powerful man who was not only popular with the liberal media but also was linked to several powerful left wing lobbies. He pretty much figured that was the reason for this assignment.

Slider had problems pulling this one off as the man was never alone and always attracting attention. He was popular and well known in the greater Seattle area. Slider always weighed the risk involved but became frustrated with his inability to isolate the victim. He decided to take a chance and get it over with. He followed him one night into a noisy, crowded gay bar just outside the city limits. As usual the man drove to the bar with several friends. They made a grand entrance into the bar.

Slider walked by once and checked for surveillance cameras. The bar catered to the gay community but had a reputation as being a cover for clientele who were straight by day and gay by night. After he entered he discovered that the lighting was poor, probably on purpose and the bar was packed. It was two or three deep at the bar and the tables were all full. This was good for him as he could sort of blend in. He located the victim and ordered a drink which he never touched. He paid with cash and noted that the bar tender grabbed his 20 and a handful of others as he snaked his way to the cash register. The change was left next to the drink. After about 10 minutes the target went by himself to the bathroom. He must have been drinking prior to this bar visit as he went right to a stall and started puking his guts out. Slider checked, nobody else in the bathroom and he softly pushed the stall door open. The latch was broken so the door did not need to be forced. He shot him once in the back of the head while the man was on his knees retching up who knows what. Slider had prepared for this and had a silencer on the end of a 22 caliber automatic pistol. The "company" always sent him out well prepared. Slider calmly walked out the bathroom, negotiated the crowded atmosphere and made it to the front door and into the night. The loud music was almost deafening and he could still hear it as he walked down the street to the rental car parked about two blocks away. Little did he know that he was back into the city limits before the body was discovered. The next morning he was on an early flight out of Seattle and he picked up a newspaper at the airport. It was an early edition and it was short on details of the murder. There was enough in the newspaper article that he knew this was about his "assignment" and the information he later picked up on the internet provided the rest of the details.

Chapter Eighteen

In early January 2017 John Price spoke at the main campus of the University of Central Florida in Orlando. His first engagement for the University at the Daytona campus had been a success and he was invited back at a much higher fee. John couldn't believe it. Some of the questions asked at Daytona in November had been tough but his research of the war pulled him through and made him more comfortable fielding the questions. John was careful and made sure he was consistent and never contradicted himself regarding the book and the topic. Vietnam always brought out passionate opinions both for and against the conflict. He never wavered about the fact that the book was fiction but admitted that there is always a shred truth in fiction.

Today's crowd was a little more challenging, more teaching staff and a few administrators. Most were just curious and some of the writing students wanted the novelty of meeting a bestselling author. The attention always stroked Price's ego. After the speaking engagement and a question and answer period he was even invited by an assistant department head to have dinner and drinks with a few of her colleagues on the University's dime.

Price accepted and although a little uneasy that he would be grilled further he was put at ease when the topics stayed off his book. They were more interested in any future projects he was working on. Price deferred stating that he didn't like to discuss ideas until he was pretty far into the project. To his surprise most of the staff present agreed on his strategy and one teaching assistant even went as far as to say she recommended the same to her students. All of this attention over a manuscript found on a lap top that he had obtained at a flea market.

Price couldn't believe how lucky he was. While on vacation with friends in early 2014 he went to a large flea market near Webster, Florida. The flea market housed numerous booths and tables that sold just about anything imaginable. Produce, firearms, used clothing, antiques, food, beverages and even electronic equipment. He discovered a fairly new Dell Laptop at a table that had an unusual mix of articles for sale. The proprietor didn't look like a computer type, he was middle aged, overweight, well inked and sported a long beard fashioned into a braid. Most of the other wares were used paperbacks, NASCAR memorabilia, and a collection of trucker baseball caps. He even had a used 12 gauge shotgun on the table. He was anxious to deal and Price offered 50 bucks and the dealer turned him down, requesting 100. Price and his friends walked away but on their way past on the other side of the aisle the bearded one signaled him over. After a short exchange the man settled for 75. Price thought it was a pretty good bargain and the guy even threw in a charging device and a couple of thumb drives.

Not being a computer guy himself Price never even took a look at the Dell until after his vacation. He asked a friend who had extensive computer knowledge to access the laptop. There was a password but his friend was able to get it open. He told Price that it had not been used for personal data such as bank accounts, bill pay or internet purchases. He told him that the only thing in the memory were some writing documents and some notes about meetings. Nothing that interested Price's IT friend. He told Price to search around the documents and once they were checked out everything could easily be deleted. His friend referred to the Dell as almost clean.

Price searched around and found a manuscript in Word that had no title. It was divided into three parts and consisted of just under 60,000 words. Price read the document in its entirety and was impressed at not only the subject matter but the writing style. He put the laptop aside for a few weeks and thought about the content. He decided to take a chance and finish the work of the author.

Although Price's writing skills were average he had a knack for editing and knew enough to make slight changes to the text. He carefully massaged the story and blended some of his own ideas into what would become a best-selling novel. He combed all through the meeting notes to make sure that there were no references to the manuscript in the notes. The actual document itself appeared to be almost complete, but not edited. There was no information about the writer on the Dell other than his name, the first names of four others in the group and that the meetings were held in Texas.

Price googled Rick Kname and traced him to William Frederick Kname. He found the obituary and realized that he had a dead man's work.

Price played a waiting game. He didn't rush the project and carefully edited and scrutinized the altered manuscript so that there were enough differences to eliminate any doubt as to whether or not his work was original. After about a year he submitted the book to a publisher. The rest was history. The book was published in the early fall of 2015 and made the New York Times best sellers list by the end of the year. Price's life changed drastically and the more notoriety he gained the less he thought about the real author of the book. After all he was dead and according to the obituary was survived only by a niece and a granddaughter.

Chapter Nineteen

Olivia played phone tag with Jim Vanderkelen early in February 2017. It seemed he was always busy when she was free and vice a versa. When she finally caught him he agreed to meet with her. He was blunt on the phone and indicated that the prevailing theory that her grandfather was the victim of a professional hit was most likely true. He also said that he had no additional information or theories about the crime not contained in his report. He did agree to see her if she wished. It seemed as though he was aggravated on the phone but Olivia figured she would meet him anyway. She had entered Steele in agility trials near Tampa in March so she made the arrangements around the trial dates. Her new rescue project JD went to Kim's for safekeeping while she was at the trials. When she dropped her off she kidded Kim with the "what goes around comes around" time worn expression but she knew that her aunt didn't mind watching the dog.

Vanderkelen lived in Trilby, a small community along route 98 between Dade City and Ridge Manor. His house sat back off the road and the property was tree lined and shaded from the hot Florida sun. It backed up to a canal that bordered a county exercise path and recreation area. The path actually stretched 12 miles according to the marker at the entrance to one of the parking lots. It was a sunny pleasant afternoon and the exercise path was busy with bike riders, runners and walkers. Vanderkelen's house was a modest, well maintained frame home with grey clapboard siding trimmed in white. A large utility shed and a detached two car garage sat at the end of the gravel driveway. The lawn was well manicured and she noticed a basketball hoop and small concrete court adjacent to the garage and shed. As she drove down the driveway she could hear a dog barking and Steele lifted his head up in the backseat, awakened from is nap on the ride from Mims.

Vanderkelen came outside through a side door, which led to a small patio containing a redwood picnic table and chairs. Vanderkelen was tall, well over 6 foot, medium build with sandy colored short cropped hair. He was casually dressed in tan cargo shorts, a faded blue Tampa Bay Lightning t shirt and flip flops. He had a pair of Oakley sunglasses propped up on his forehead. A small black short haired dog followed him outside and ran towards the back of the yard. Vanderkelen smiled, waived and directed her to park in front of the garage. She was surprised as he appeared more affable than the person she had talked to on the phone.

Like Vanderkelen, Olivia was casually dressed. She had recently had her hair cut short and there wasn't enough to pull back. She covered her head with a brand new Daytona Kennel Club baseball cap she bought at the flea market in Volusia. She didn't belong but the club had a neat design on the hat, a greyhound running at full stride. Faded orange lightweight fishing shorts, blue Adidas t- shirt and Brooks running shoes with no socks. Vanderkelen looked her up and down and broke out in an ear to ear smile. She wasn't put off, as his glance wasn't offending, more like just appreciating the scenery. He pointed to the picnic table and chairs and then spoke.

"Have a seat, I got ice tea, water and coffee on in the house, choose your poison."

Olivia opened the hatch to the FJ which was parked in the shade. She made sure Steele was comfortable and he had fresh water. She took him from the back seat and told him to jump up into his crate, which was in the cargo space behind the back seat. She left the hatch door open. Being a good traveler he was asleep almost as fast as he woke up when she pulled in to the driveway.

"I'll have ice tea, thanks."

Vanderkelen went into the house and returned to the picnic table with a pitcher of ice tea and two glasses.

"That's a handsome dog you got there. What is he, you know what breed."

"He's a German Pinscher, we are on our way to an agility trial weekend near Tampa."

Vanderkelen looked back at the FJ and commented, "he looks well trained, maybe you could give my little one there some lessons," he pointed to the small black dog who was now laying in the grass chewing on what looked like an old piece of tree branch.

"I'm not really a trainer, just trying to be a handler, but he, his name is Steele, is good. He's fast and brave."

Vanderkelen got right to the point. It wasn't like he was in a hurry, more like he wanted to get the subject of the visit off of his plate.

"I hope you don't end up thinking this was a waste of time, let me give you my spiel and then you can ask questions."

Vanderkelen's narrative described how he became involved in the case and he reiterated everyone's theory that the murder was a professional hit and would probably remain unsolved. There was always the possibility that the hit man would make a mistake somewhere down the road but whoever hired him would kill him rather than allow him to make a deal with authorities. The mistake could be a disclosure to protect someone else, or variations thereof.

Now that he was retired and a PI he occasionally looked back at the case, he had a habit of wanting to solve what others felt was unsolvable. He pointed out a few areas that were not looked into and wondered why nobody ever actually tried to interview friends of her grandfather's from North Texas. He also knew that Rick had worked part time for a PI and wondered why that lead was not followed up on. He stopped short of blaming anyone, and never mentioned the reputation of the original detective who caught the case. In short he was less accusatory than Woodruff regarding the way the investigation was handled.

Olivia described her conversations with Linda Rossi and explained what Rossi had disclosed about her grandfather's writing and the novel published by John Price. She described how the novel was about Vietnam and wondered out loud if something her grandfather had done in Vietnam could have caused his murder. Vanderkelen told her that it was highly unlikely that it would take all those years for Rick to be murdered over something that happened in Vietnam. He also said that Spader didn't say much about their service together. Vanderkelen went on to say that from his experience most Vietnam vets, or any vets for that matter, never talked much about war. Spader had also described Rick's job with Pacific Engineering and it seemed to him it was pretty routine follow up work for a contract they had with the Department of Defense Police. He understood that Rick didn't even have to carry a weapon for the job. Vanderkelen even made a few remarks about Spader, calling him a "character." He asked how well Olivia knew him. She went on to say that she had never met him but had been trying to contact him.

Olivia ask a few questions and said that she wanted to take some time and look into her grandfather's death herself. Vanderkelen didn't seem surprised stating that she would not have come all the way out here or gone to talk to Woodruff if she wasn't interested in looking at it herself. He offered that she could call him at any time on his cell if she needed any direction or help.

Just before she left Vanderkelen's youngest daughter, Ashley, age 9 arrived home from school. Vanderkelen introduced them and Ashley told her father that she didn't have softball practice today and was given a lift home by their neighbor who also had a daughter who played on the team. Ashley said that she called her mom and got permission to ride home with Mrs. Elliot. Vanderkelen smiled and offered Ashley praise for being careful. Ashley went inside and Vanderkelen described his retirement and sometime PI job as being a Mr. Mom. His wife still taught and coached at a local High School as she changed jobs after they got married. He avoided any more details about his family situation, figuring Woodruff had probably told her or at least pointed her in the direction of his past. He figured that Olivia at least looked him up on the internet and probably discovered much of the background regarding his demotion.

Just before she left Vanderkelen repeated and stressed one point from is narrative.

"You know, Spader said that Rick did some work for a Private Investigator in Dallas for a few years before he was killed. Spader said that he had a license in Texas and mainly took an occasional surveillance job or interview in the far North Texas area to save the PI in Dallas the trip up from the city. If anything you should talk to Spader. I don't think he would talk over the phone or by e mail, didn't seem to be the tech type. Might have to make trip to Southern Oklahoma to see him.

"Hey I hear Oklahoma is pretty nice, an underrated and often overlooked place. Spader will talk to you, I got the impression he and your grandfather were really close. Here, he gave me his address and cell number."

Vanderkelen printed Spader's information on the back of one of his PI business cards. Olivia already had the information but allowed Vanderkelen to transcribe it anyway. She also wanted his business card in case she ever needed to contact him. After all he had offered.

Olivia and Jim Vanderkelen said their goodbyes and Olivia and Steele headed towards the Tampa area and the arena where the trials were being held.

Chapter Twenty

May 2017, Clifford Nauvana entered his efficiency apartment near the Portland suburb of Hillsboro. It was early evening, chilly with intermittent drizzle. Clifford wished the weather were more spring like, as he hated the cold and rain. He threw his worn canvas jacket on the couch and shook the rain off of his faded Mariners baseball cap. He had just returned from a beer run. He stored the 12 pack of Olympia in the fridge and surveyed the contents for food. The apartment was one of four in a rundown house located in what was a previously affluent neighborhood. The area had long since deteriorated from neglect and the changing demographics of the area. Apartment 3, second floor rear. When the house was converted to apartments it had received the full treatment outside, but the conversion inside was less impressive. The years had taken its toll on the exterior though, and the once clean vinyl siding was now dirty and loose in several places. The landlord spared little effort or money maintaining the house.

Clifford cracked open a cold one and sat down on the threadbare daybed and turned on the 10 year old Sony 19 inch TV. His apartment was a one room efficiency with a small kitchen that contained old appliances from an era gone by. The fridge and the stove didn't even match on either brand or color. The bathroom had a toilet, shower stall, sink and small vanity. The walls of the bathroom were papered, now peeling and showing signs of mold because of the moisture and lack of an exhaust fan. The living room walls hadn't had a coat of paint in years. The furniture was mismatched, all of a Goodwill variety.

Clifford figured that although he didn't have much he at least wasn't homeless. All one had to do was take a trip through Portland and view the growing homeless community. Clifford took a few gulps of beer and removed his worn Nike running shoes. His socks both had holes in the toes. Portland area was a far cry from San Antonio Texas, where he grew up. He turned on the TV hoping to catch the news and maybe the Mariners game.

Clifford was the youngest of three children. His two older sisters, both in their 70's lived in Texas. His mother and father were deceased. Clifford's Mexican American father met his Canadian mother while stationed at Elmendorf Air Force base in Alaska. His dad opted for a career in the military and spent most of his enlistment stationed at Lackland AFB in San Antonio. Although not exactly a marriage made in heaven they survived and did a relatively good job of raising all three children. Both sisters had families and kept their Texas roots.

Clifford was shy and had few friends growing up. As a young child he was often picked on and teased. His father was good to Clifford and he encouraged him to make friends. But they were never what you could call close. He was however, close to his mother and had inherited her good looks. She was born in Canada. She was part French Canadian and part Native American on her mother's side. Although slightly built he was very handsome and possessed strikingly dark features and a muscular frame. He was good at sports and an above average student but his shy nature got in his way. He could never get up the nerve to go out for sports teams in High School. One thing about him though was he was a favorite of the High School girls. He never let his good looks get in the way of his popularity with the females.

Upon graduating from High School he immediately joined the Army on three year enlistment. Within five months of enlistment he landed in country, Vietnam. After his tour he was assigned to the training brigade at Ft. Lewis Washington. He remained there until his discharge from the Army. He always felt sorry for the recruits he helped prepare for their tours in Vietnam. As the drill sergeant's used to say "Ft. Lewis is about as close to Vietnam as you can get without being there." They, the recruits, all pretty much knew their fate.

After his discharge he stayed in the Pacific Northwest. He met both his ex- wives in the area. One in Washington and one in Oregon. The years passed with two divorces, two stints in rehab and more than a dozen jobs between periods of unemployment. This was the road for Clifford to his present existence.

Clifford's dismal job record wasn't because he was a bad employee it was because of his drinking and poor choices regarding women. Sober he was actually a good worker who could be trusted. The drinking led to absenteeism which in turn led to the pink slips. Currently he lived on his social security check and a small pension that was vested from a cable television company. He managed ten years there before being let go. It was just enough for a meager vested pension. Clifford just made it with three months to spare. He drove a beat up Ford Ranger pickup, had little in the way of savings and dressed in grunge chic. The drinking aged him but he still was pretty fit for his 66 years, had a full head of salt and pepper hair and maintained some of that handsome aura. He constantly wondered why he never returned to the southwest as he hated the Pacific Northwest and especially the weather. His contact with his two sisters was infrequent and his list of friends was nonexistent. Luckily both ex- wives had moved on and didn't bother him for support payments. Neither wife had a child by him.

Clifford opened another beer and used the remote to find the Mariners game from the east coast. Two more pulls on the beer and he returned to the frig searching for something to make a sandwich with. He settled for a day old slice of pizza left over from yesterday's dinner. No microwave, so rather than heat it up in the stove he ate it cold.

Although he hadn't seen anyone from his days in the Army he read in the paper about the death of Rick Kname. Kname had been good to him and insulated his from the realities of their mission in Vietnam. He knew that Rick had his back and would shoulder the blame if there were any problems or fallout from what Rick called "the realities of the job." The most important thing was that Rick and Eddie Spader both had confidence in his abilities. After he heard about Rick's death he was able to locate Eddie Spader through the internet at a local public library. He had the ability to master tech issues, but not the means to own a computer or subscribe to an internet connection. His television reception was from a master antenna on the roof of the house that made up the four apartments. He wrote him on several occasions and Spader tried in vain to get Clifford to move to Oklahoma and get on his feet there. Clifford just wasn't able to make the move. The Mariners were losing. Clifford lit up a cigarette opened another beer, his third, and changed the channel to an old sitcom on one of the local off the air channels.

Chapter Twenty-One

January 1971, three years removed from the Tet offensive of 1968 the mission of the US forces in Vietnam had changed. The escalation of replacements had subsided as the military was facing criticism from ever growing antiwar groups back in the US. Protests had increased and social the unrest was more prevalent. The US military had started a program that they called Vietnamization. Vietnamization was a complete reversal of policy regarding the US involvement in the war. The burden of fighting the war had been the sole responsibility of the US troops. Little thought or effort had been given to actually training the South Vietnam Army to handle the bulk of the fighting. The transition was projected to be slow, to insure that the ARVN (Army of the Republic of Vietnam) were prepared to shoulder the responsibility. If successful the US troops could assume a backup role and start a slow withdrawal of US support in the country. One of the key objectives of Vietnamization was to make sure that the village and hamlet leaders were not supporting the Viet Cong and the NVA (North Vietnam Army). It was the classic democracy versus Communism pitch. Many felt that this was the justification for getting involved in Vietnam in the first place. Some questioned as to why the US didn't initially let the ARVN assume most of the responsibility. One high ranking official put it this way. "It's like a father buying his son a set of golf clubs, assuming he will be interested in playing golf. Once the father discovers that the son doesn't like or show an interest in golf he starts using the clubs himself. Afterwards he likes it so much he buys himself a set of clubs and develops an ongoing interest in golf. Meanwhile the set he bought his son sits dormant in the garage. He continues to play and establishes relationships with friends who golf and doesn't let his son participate. Eventually the son becomes completely disinterested and the father wonders why."

Rick, Eddie Spader and Clifford had been sent back into an area near the Cambodian border. The Tet offensive had been mostly mounted and launched by infiltration of NVA, supplies and refreshed Viet Cong from the sanctuary of Cambodia. The village of An Ninh had become a problem because of an informant that the ARVN's and the US troops operating in the area thought was friendly but came to believe that he had been leaking intelligence to the VC.

Rick often shared more of the details of the hits with Spader than with Clifford. Eddie was a volunteer to the unit and liked working with Rick. Clifford had more or less been drafted into the unit, which in a way was a compliment, considering the responsibility that came with the assignments. The more they worked together the more Rick shared with Clifford. He had demonstrated an ability to remain calm under fire and always carried out his orders. All three knew the details on this mission.

They had been to An Ninh three times in a four week period and Rick had become frustrated. Each time the target had eluded them and most likely had sought refuge in Cambodia. Rick speculated that their target was not the only communist friendly man in the village. He was also curious about men the targets age who were not in the military. He figured most young men served on one side or the other.

The fourth time looked no better. It was early February and it looked as though he had eluded them again. Rick attempted some dialogue with the locals but it was apparent that the target was well known and well liked. Several of the villagers who had previously said they knew the informant now denied knowing him. Not only did Rick catch them in a lie but he also noticed that the village appeared to be less populated than the three previous visits. This led Rick to believe that the village was a lot less friendly than HQ's intelligence thought.

Since they believed that they had missed him again they had radioed for pickup outside the village. HDQ's replied that a resupply Huey would pick them up at prearranged coordinates within an hour. It was early in the day and they started to hump towards the rendezvous point. A series of paths crisscrossed a checkerboard of rice paddies and they spaced themselves far enough apart as not to become an easy target for a sniper. As they entered a tree lined area with Eddie in the lead they stumbled upon 4 or 5 VC who were casually moving in the opposite direction at a Y in the path. They must not have been unaware of the presence of the three GI's as they were making a lot of noise, smoking and talking very loudly. Eddie stopped and concealed himself off of the path and signaled back to Rick. Rick turned back towards Clifford and pointed forward, placing his forefinger at his lips and motioned him off to the same side as Eddie. Eddie checked his M16, made sure the safety was off and moved further away from the right side of the path. It was almost like slow motion. Then everything happened in real time. Rick had moved off the path to the left and Clifford moved took cover off of the right side almost directly behind Eddie. The two VC at the rear of the column turned back. They noticed movement in the cover and started to fire in the direction of Eddie. Eddie fired back and got the rear man dead on and hit the next one in line but he was able to move away, but took the alternate path on the Y. The firing ended as quickly as it started and

Rick and Clifford moved slowly along opposite the sides of the path towards Eddie.

Rick watched another VC come back to the dead body and he appeared to remove a satchel from his body. Rick pointed in his direction and Eddie and Clifford both fired on him and he slumped over the body. They could hear what sounded like two more running away on the opposite path leading away from the Y. They moved very slowly towards the body at the base of the Y and discovered that he was dead. Two other VC were also dead but the satchel lay on the path between the bodies. Rick carefully removed the satchel, making sure that it was not wired for explosives. It was later determined that the satchel contained intelligence information that the VC had gathered on US and ARVN battalions operating in the area. The bonus factor was that it was also determined that one of the dead VC was their target. Rick recognized him from the picture of him he had seen when briefed on the mission. Rick told them both that he was their man. He was out of range for Rick's Ithaca but either Eddie or Clifford had taken him with a 16. At this point Rick was pretty sure that Clifford understood what their missions were all about.

They continued towards the pickup site where they caught the resupply Huey and were transported to the base camp.

❧

Chapter Twenty-Two

Rick and his two man unit continued to work the area near the Cambodian border as the war effort in 1971 dragged on. It was early June and Rick was waiting for orders from command as to whether or not his assignment was going to be extended. He had heard that the higher ups were considering a new strategy to neutralize the influence of the NVA, the Viet Cong and Viet Cong sympathizers. It was still called Vietnamization but the present form was going to be modified. The strategy of the NVA hadn't changed as they still continued to resupply the VC along the Cambodian border and continued their effort to re- educate the neutral and pro American villages and hamlets.

Clifford was looking forward to his DEROS (destination estimate to return from overseas) date in July. Eddie said he would extend and stay if he could remain with Rick. Rick was pretty sure that he would rotate back in September if the current mission wasn't extended. Rick had never been keen on the chain of command and taking orders. He liked the fact that he and his two man group could just do their job and stay under the radar of the commanders. It also was to his liking that when in base camp they were left alone by commanders and support personnel. It was an understood hands off policy. Almost no one really knew the function of the small unit anyway. Rick knew there were rumors about them, but he never paid the "talk" around the base camp any mind. He had complied with their rules during his first tour as an infantry squad leader, this tour he made the rules.

A battalion sized operation was initiated in late June. Rick, Clifford and Eddie were dispatched to join one of the companies sweeping through a cluster of villages and hamlets near the Cambodian border. The operation also included two intelligence officers, both spoke Vietnamese. Command had decided to attempt to flush out VC cadre operating in the area with a show of force. This would be the last time Rick, Eddie and Clifford would work together.

The company encountered heavy resistance but American casualties were light and they were able to round up a few suspects. Attempts to interrogate were unsuccessful. The two intelligence officers assigned to the operation took the lead on the interrogations. Rick knew that this was a sign that his role was no longer needed. He sealed it in his mind that officers were going to take over his role and the philosophy of the tactics had changed. He figured that command wanted more control and substituting Rick for officers made sense to them. Rick was able to observe that the two intelligence officer's command of Vietnamese, despite their advanced training, was not much better than his. He also questioned their interviewing skills and lack of field experience. It didn't matter command would go ahead with the new policy. Rick, Eddie and Clifford remained with the company until the sweep of the area was completed. Intelligence was able to obtain only limited information as to the operations of the communist along the Cambodian border. After the operation was completed the battalion returned to base camp in July. Rick, Eddie and Clifford knew that their purpose as a unit had expired. Clifford rotated back to the US in late July and finished his enlistment in a training unit at Fort Lewis Washington. Rick returned stateside in September and was reassigned to a basic training company at Ft. Bragg, North Carolina. Spader extended his tour for 6 more months and was assigned to a base camp headquarters company supply unit. He would eventually DEROS in the spring of 1972 and he was assigned to Ft. Sam Houston, Texas.

Chapter Twenty-Three

Olivia continued to run Steele, work at the car dealership and help Aunt Kim, life as usual. Every day the mystery surrounding her Grandfather surfaced in her mind. She couldn't shake her curiosity. She tried to reach out to Franklin "Eddie" Spader via e mail a few times between April and July 2017. Spader never responded and Olivia was temporarily discouraged. She thought about making a trip to Oklahoma and she had his address from her contacts with both Vanderkelen and Detective Woodruff. She wondered if just dropping in on him was a good idea.

Life in Central Florida had seemed to become stagnate. She still owned the house in Texas that had been part of her grandfather's will. The house was in good condition and located in an area where the property values were increasing. After the disputes were settled she thought about selling it but changed her mind and leased it through a rental and property maintenance company. The extra income was helpful and she was advised that the area was ripe for growth and property would only appreciate. The current tenants, according to the management company, were taking reasonable care of the house but were on a month to month arrangement because the husband was getting transferred. They were considering a move as his new work location was too far to commute. In the back of her mind she thought about picking up and moving to Texas. She had done research on the area and discovered that the job market was good and the cost of living was reasonable.

She wasn't involved in any relationships and figured that maybe the change would be good for her.

Chapter Twenty-Four

In September 2017 John Price received a call from his agent, Lauren Holmes. Lauren and John rarely spoke, but recently Lauren had been pressing him about where he was on another novel. She lived by the saying strike when the iron is hot. Although John hadn't done much he kept telling her he was re working an old project and he would keep her informed. Actually other than enjoying the popularity and perks from Mind of the Assassin he had done nothing. Usually he left her calls go to voice mail and hoped she didn't follow up. But on this sunny afternoon he was sitting on is deck, smoking and drinking some Heinekens and enjoying the view of the Banana River.

"Hey, Lauren what's up, been a while since I've heard from you."

"John, if you would listen to your voice mails you would know I have been calling, don't play dumb on me here, ok."

"Ok Lauren, usually if I'm working on something I let the messages go, then just never get around to it. Plus I've been having some work done on this house, been focused on that stuff, you know stuff with the contractor."

"Ok John, now that I've got you wanted to chat and see how you were doing on the new book, also got something else I wanted to run by you."

"Lauren, I've given up on that project for the time being, I'm just starting something fresh, pretty much in the thought process, only have a few ideas down on my computer, want me to give you a preview?"

"John, you're bullshitting me, you have first novel itis, pretty common, just play it straight with me, ok. I know damn well you haven't been working on anything. Let's move on to topic number two."

"Ok, shoot, by the way am I in trouble?"

"John, your book is highly successful, the paperback distribution is doing very well so you have time to ride the wave for a while but listen here is the other issue. I have been receiving calls from a teacher in Texas, her name is Bobbi Greene, ever heard of her?"

"Lauren, no why, what is this about."

"John, has she ever contacted you?"

"No, I never heard of her."

"Ok, listen I ignored her calls for over a year, she was sporadic and not very aggressive at first. Lately she has upped the ante a little, and I finally relented and returned her call. She claims to have been in a writing group with a man named Frederick, I think that was the name. She called him Rick, his last name was Kname, pronounced like the word name. She said that Mr. Kname was murdered in 2013, actually in Florida. She said that he had been writing a book and had read parts of it to her group. She went on to say that his book resembled your novel. Now I'm not sure what she is driving at here, what her motive is, but I sort of played it off and said I would talk to you about it. Before I called I had one of my staff do a little research."

"Ok Lauren, research for what, what is the punch line here?"

"No punch line, the guy, Kname, was a Vietnam vet, spent about 20 years in the army, worked for the government for a while and after retirement worked part time for a private investigator in the Dallas area. This Greene women lives north of Dallas. And even more interesting Kname's granddaughter lives very close to you. She actually lives in Mims, I googled it, same county you live in. So, any knowledge of what I'm talking about?"

"No, I never heard of any of the people, come on Lauren what are you driving at."

"Plagiarism, ok, we have to play this very carefully, a lot of stuff here I don't know, but if you have any contact here or you are holding out on me, let me know. No bullshit John, serious stuff. A few years ago I had another situation with an author I represented. As it turned out, the person making the allegations had a hard on for the guy, and made it up. So I'm not jumping to conclusions here. I'll have your back but if you fuck with me, lie to me I'll throw you under the bus in a heartbeat."

"No, I don't know any of these people, I did not plagiarize this. I read a lot about Vietnam, there is lots of stuff out there, you know, books good and bad. I also talked to a few vets. Got their input, was up front with them, they knew I was writing a book. Anyway I wrote the story and that's about it."

"John, she is going to get back and I suspect may try and call my bluff, If she calls you for any reason, listen to the voice mail and get back to me, don't talk to her, no excuses."

"Ok Lauren, keep me posted. Like I said before are we, or should I say am I in trouble here."

"John, sounds like you are worried about something, this is why we have lawyers. Anyway, start producing, or I may become very suspicious, not necessarily about the call but about your abilities."

"Look, no knowledge of this stuff at all, that's it."

"Right John, you better not be hiding anything, goodbye."

Price hung up and started to worry a little. He opened another beer, walked back out to the deck, lit another cigarette and started to think that he may have to tell Lauren where he got the idea for the book.

Chapter Twenty-Five

About 85 miles north from Dallas on interstate 75 just past Dennison, Texas you cross the Red River into Oklahoma. The area is mostly rural with the exception of the Choctaw Casino and entertainment complex about 9 miles north of the bridge. Exit 75 about 5 miles further north and you enter the town of Durant. Durant is a small town in Bryant County about 15 miles north of the Red River. Take a left on Main Street in Durant and head west on route 70. About half way to Lake Texoma is a small country road, Mission Road, it intersects route 70. The area is interspersed with horse and cattle ranches of various sizes. About a mile north on the left side of Mission Road is the small brick and stone ranch house of Eddie Spader. The house sits back off the road on a 3 plus acre plot of flat land. At the end of a gravel driveway a metal car port is attached to the right of the house. The car port protects a well maintained 2001 Toyota pickup truck from the hail storms common in North Texas and Southern Oklahoma. A large metal utility building sits off to the right and houses a small tractor, maintenance equipment and various hand and power tools. It also houses his pristine 1993 Ford Bronco. Outside the building is a horse trailer. There is a small barn adjacent to the utility building and contains Eddie's two horses, both rescues from rodeo enterprises. A chestnut mare and a grey gelding.

Spader lives alone on this property which he purchased in the late 90's. He lived in a trailer on the property until he had the house built in 2006. The metal utility building was added a few years later when he sold the trailer. The barn was a project he worked on for years, he actually built it himself. After his retirement from a job with the State of Oklahoma he enjoys a casual life style. He occasionally takes odd jobs for cash on the as a hand on local ranches. After a life time of failed relationships he has pretty much given up on women. He does have an on again off again relationship but it is more off than on. He does remarkably well keeping the house presentable and sustaining himself. He actually turned into a pretty good cook by necessity when his various girlfriends left for greener pastures. Although his pension is modest he supplements it with social security benefits and his occasional part time work. He has no outstanding debt and was smart enough to save during his years working for the state. With no mortgage, the low cost of living in Oklahoma and no outstanding debt he pretty much can live as he pleases.

The inside of his house is a mixture of furniture bought at yard and estate sales. All of which he reconditioned himself. The motif is genuine western art in picture frames he obtained at yard sales, all reconditioned by himself. Satellite TV and high speed internet allow him to catch up on sports, news and weather. Occasionally he takes a trip to Norman and takes in an OU sporting event live. He is a big OU football fan and follows the Texas Rangers during baseball season.

It's early October 2017 and his 6 ft. 225lb. frame is covered by an old pair of Levi jeans, well- worn cowboy boots, and a black pocket t shirt. His thick gray hair is pulled back in a pony-tail and is covered by a faded and sweat stained blue Texas Rangers baseball hat. He has about a three day growth of facial hair and a small gold hoop dangles from his left ear. His well-developed forearms and biceps are covered with tattoos representing various phases of his life.

Eddie has been bothered by some recent phone calls regarding his deceased friend Rick Kname. First it was detectives and a private investigator from Florida and more recently Rick's granddaughter. But more puzzling was a call from a women who stated she was a friend of Rick's and used to be in a writing group with him. Eddie wasn't aware of any writing group although Rick did mention taking some courses for fiction writing at the University of North Texas. Rick and Eddie never discussed the writing. Eddie sat on the porch smoked a cigarette and opened an early can of beer. He checked his watch, it was 12:40. Must be 5 o'clock somewhere he said to himself.

Eddie cooperated with the detectives and answered their questions about the murder of his friend. One thing he never did was speculate or give his opinion of why Rick was murdered. He figured it wasn't his job to investigate and felt that what they were looking for was not the obvious. He knew that they would never find the killer, it was a contract job, done by a professional. He had some ideas as to why, but they were only ideas. He definitely knew it had nothing to do with Vietnam, if that was the reason he would have been killed a long time ago. In his opinion nobody wanted to deal with Vietnam anyway. Especially the politicians, they were quick to get America involved in wars, as long as it wasn't their kids who had to fight them.

Chapter Twenty-Six

Early November 2017 Slider was living in a suburb of Myrtle Beach, SC. He had not been given an assigned for about two months and he was enjoying the climate and easy pace of life in South Carolina. He went to the ocean and surf fished in the mornings and spent the afternoons relaxing outside his leased condo. His last two assignments had been pretty easy, and on one he was only to act as a back-up and actually didn't have to kill anyone. The other "actor" as they called them was the primary and as usual he knew him only by his code name. This told him that the primary was probably new or the company had some doubts about him and they wanted to make sure the kill went off without a hitch.

His new assignment was in the Philadelphia area and the target was a women. 20 years on the job and he had never been assigned to kill a women. He wasn't all that comfortable with it but couldn't under any circumstances reveal any weaknesses to his employer. Word around the business was that only the strong survive and those who hesitated, or made too many mistakes were themselves a target. Another thing about the assignment it meant he had to return to the area where he had spent the early years of his life. Even though the target worked in Philadelphia she lived about 60 miles south of where he spent years in an adolescent residential facility. He rarely dwelled on his past, something he had no control over. When he did think about his early years he often wondered if his background was part of the reason he ended up in this profession.

The target was a lawyer, she worked for a Philadelphia law firm but lived in a suburb in Camden County New Jersey. He was given an extensive background history on her and as usual he did his own research on her. The additional information he obtained usually helped him with the job and sometimes it shed more light on why the target was actually designated to be hit. From the information gathered by himself and that supplied by his employer he knew it was going to a difficult job. He was also told by his employer that he was allowed extra time to complete the assignment. This was rare also, as usually the hits were directed to take place in short time frames. This told him two things, one the target was a priority and two failing to complete the assignment would put him in jeopardy. One thing he didn't know was there was a connection between this target and a previous kill of his. Slider made travel and lodging arrangements and arrived in Philadelphia a few days before Thanksgiving 2017.

Chapter Twenty-Seven

nnie Kinser was always a wallflower. As a child she never got the attention her older brother got. After all he was a local high school football hero and that bought much attention to himself and the family. Annie grew up in the north eastern suburbs of Philadelphia, Bucks County. She never listened to those who criticized her and underestimated her abilities. She never allowed being overshadowed by her brother to get in her way. After high school she attended Temple University and after graduation worked three years as a para legal at a Philadelphia law firm. While working as a para legal she enrolled in the night law program at Temple.

After attaining her law degree and passing the Pennsylvania bar she took a job with the Bucks County public defender's office. The experience helped her gain confidence and enhanced her resume. Her work as a para legal also helped her gain employment with the Philadelphia law firm where she started her work career. They were happy to have her back as an attorney. Annie's career moved slowly, like most lawyers she got little in the way of trial work and ended up preparing and researching cases for senior attorneys. As time went by she started to get trial work and her abilities and self-confidence improved. Eventually she started getting higher profile cases. Also as she aged her physical appearance became more pleasing, some would refer to her as a late bloomer.

Philadelphia was the location of a trial where a well- known physician was accused of performing full term abortions. The doctor was convicted of murder for ending the life of five infants after they were delivered full term in his clinic. The trial and subsequent conviction caused friction between pro-life and pro- choice groups in the area. Annie's law firm was chosen by a pro-life group who contended that they were being targeted and harassed by pro-choice advocates. They further stated in their grievance that the liberal politicians in the city did little to protect their right to state and demonstrate their beliefs.

Much to her surprise Annie was chosen as the lead attorney over more senior men and women lawyers in the firm. Her hard work and abilities had drawn the attention and confidence of the top administrators in the firm. This was a very high profile and important case for the firm and moreover an important and highly contested subject nationwide. Even the liberal mayor of Philadelphia had to walk back his comments when he was overheard saying that they (the firm) could have chosen more capable attorney for the case. He added "and even a better looking one." He ended up having to apologize for his statement, something out of character for him and his liberal cohorts. It didn't matter anyway, Annie had developed a thick skin and the comments and criticism only made her work harder.

Chapter Twenty-Eight

John Price had a change of heart. After a few months of worrying about his conversation with his agent he decided that even though the bulk of his novel came from the found laptop, he really never did anything illegal, at least not in his mind on purpose. He even rationalized that if this work was known, even known by just a few people, how come there was no discussion about it when the writer was murdered. Also, didn't whoever sold the laptop, even look at the contents. He figured it was stolen and for no other reason than financial gain. He tried as many ways as possible to justify his work and diminish the fact that the writing sort of fell into his lap.

John called his agent in late November. He admitted that "at least" some of the work came from another source. He left out the fact that it came from a "found" laptop. He went on to state that he never considered what he did to be plagiarism or he would have never submitted the manuscript.

Lauren's response surprised him. She went on to state that she had already talked to an attorney and gave him a hypothetical situation regarding John's work. She added that the lawyer probably figured it was a real situation with maybe some facts changed. In other words she was on a fishing expedition. The lawyer played along anyway, as he was under retainer for one of the publishing firms she sent manuscripts to. The lawyer told her that proving anything would be difficult, as the supposed author, according to Lauren's version of the story, was dead. Lauren was relieved but decided to let John hang awhile, maybe he would be motivated to work. She admitted during the conversation that she expected a call from him sooner than later. Also she figured that this would help her decide whether or not John had any talent. But prior to the call she had already made a decision to dump him. She didn't let on, she figured that maybe if he sweat for a while he might be more forthcoming and dumping him would be easier.

Lauren told John that the worst possible scenario was a small cash settlement to whoever was the receiver of his estate, in this case the granddaughter. She reminded John not to discuss this with anyone and failed to disclose to him that the calls from the teacher had stopped.

With the new found information John took a deep breath and searched the internet for a list of agents. He felt even though Lauren didn't mention it she was going to dump him no matter how this played out.

Chapter Twenty-Nine

Target Annie was a bitch. Slider knew this was going to be difficult but never imagined it to be this complicated. Annie's condo in South Jersey was about a ten minute drive from the Woodcrest PATCO station. PATCO stood for Port Authority Transit Corporation. It was referred to as the high speed line and ran from stops in South Jersey to center city Philadelphia. She took PATCO to the Market Street East station in Philadelphia and walked three blocks to the office building where the law firm was located. Her schedule varied and she was putting in long hours so her commuting schedule could not be predicted.

Slider posed as a construction worker and road PATCO into the city every morning trying to establish a pattern and an opening for an opportunity to take the target. It was easy to blend in, the commuter riders were a mix of business professionals, students and workers from various construction unions. The Thanksgiving and Christmas holiday season placed a burden on his observations as there were more shoppers on the trains than usual. Just after Thanksgiving Annie disappeared from her routine. She had an occasional boyfriend and they had made plans to spend a long weekend with his family in Delaware. Slider didn't even know about the boyfriend as there was no mention of him in the information he received from his employer. He was able to establish that the boyfriend didn't live with her and rarely stayed overnight at her apartment. Even her co- workers at the law firm knew little about him.

After Thanksgiving Annie's pattern became more erratic as she prepared for the trial which was scheduled for mid-January 2018. Slider changed motels three times and had to constantly make sure that he kept a low profile on the days he was lucky enough be on the right PATCO train. He discarded any idea of trying to take her at her condo. The security was state of the art and the route from the train station was heavily traveled. There were security cameras at the PATCO station and usually there was a transit cop on site, but the parking lot was large and the lighting was poor at each extreme end. The lot was separated into a pay and non- pay area with the pay areas closest to the entrance of the terminal. The ticket office had been closed and replaced with machines to purchase the fare tickets. After the second week in December Slider decided that he was going to have to make the hit in the evening in the parking lot, preferably on a night when Annie worked late. He figured he would have to take a chance that the transit cop had either circled the lot or maybe even left briefly to get a cup of coffee. He was going to have to take a risk.

Chapter Thirty

December brought on the agility invitation in Orlando, the 15th through the 17th. Olivia and Steele had qualified again, as usual there were not a lot of German Pinschers running in agility, but they had done well and accumulated more points than the previous years. Same cast of characters and this year Olivia and Steele made it to the final round again. Steele had developed into a skilled and accurate dog. Not only was he fast and brave but now he was more focused. The agility crowd was even more envious of Olivia. Not only did they resent her lithe body and understated good looks, but now her handling skills, honed over the last two years, were a threat to them. Even though she wasn't running a Border or a Sheltie, on a good day Steele and Olivia could compete with the best of them. Today she wore plain grey Adidas running shorts, an oversized black t shirt, matching white Adidas running shoes and white ankle socks. She had a plain white baseball cap pulled over her short black hair. She sat in her stadium chair in the crating area, listening on her I phone to a medley of songs by various artists all accompanied by Duane Allman on slide guitar. The walk thru for the finals was scheduled in about an hour. Steele lounged in his crate unfazed by the yapping and barking of the various dogs crated around him.

In South Jersey Slider sat in shot and beer bar on the White Horse Pike, watching a college football game. The weather was miserable. It was cold and had rained for three straight days. Slider had picked up smoking again and was drinking more than usual. He would go outside and smoke by the front door in between draft beers. He pulled the hood up on his canvas work jacket and kicked at the sidewalk cursing as he talked to himself. The attitude to this type of climate never changed. It had been close to a month and he was running out of options for target Annie. He was going to attempt the hit earlier in the week, but she had a knack for changing her routine every time he was ready for an attempt. Despite his years on the job, his experience, and his normally cool approach he was starting to worry about how to pull this off. He knew that he had to complete this job without much more delay. Two people, 1000 miles apart with one thing in common. Unbeknownst to both of them they were going to experience major changes in their respective lives.

Olivia and Steele qualified on the final run, a hybrid course, and placed third overall out of the original 122 dogs at the 20" jump height. Olivia was surprised as several of the top handlers congratulated her and commented on how sound and fluid Steele was. Olivia smiled, glanced back at the crate, Steele had already gone to sleep, unfazed by the adulation. Olivia thought to herself, dogs never get full of themselves like people do. It amazed her at how loyal they were. One thing about Steele, he always gave her everything he had. She waited to pick up the final score card and the placement ribbon. She had broken down and purchased a polo shirt with the Agility Invitational Logo on it. She was proud of her dog, and happy with the way she had handled the pressure. The congratulations of the competitors, some of whom had never even acknowledged her, was icing on the cake. She started to pack up and get ready for the drive back to Mims.

Slider gulped one more beer, chased it with a shot of bourbon and walked outside to smoke another cigarette. The rain had now turned to sleet, he cursed, crushed the cigarette on the sidewalk. Then he started the walk to the Motel 6 down the pike. Another day in scenic South Jersey.

Chapter Thirty-One

Slider took PATCO to Philadelphia early Monday morning, Annie was on the same train but two cars ahead. Slider sat next to a middle aged man dressed in a suit and topcoat. He never took his eyes from his smart phone and didn't acknowledge Slider as he sat down. Two young women sat in the seat on the opposite side of the aisle. They were casually dressed and discussed Christmas plans. The train was crowded and a few passengers stood holding on to the hand rails. Slider wasn't masquerading as a construction worker on this morning. He was casually dressed in jeans, hiking boots, plaid flannel shirt and a lined denim jacket. He covered his head with a black watch cap. He had a 22 caliber Ruger semi- automatic pistol in an ankle holster. The weather was cold, a slight drizzle that bordered on flurries and no sign of the sun. He got off at Market Street East and managed to spot Annie as she started up the stairway to ground level. He stayed about 6 to 10 feet behind her and followed her out to the street. He then crossed the street and trailed her as she walked the three blocks to her office building. Once she entered the building he continued down Market Street. He had made up his mind that tonight was going to be the hit, he figured she might leave on time, as it was getting close to Christmas and he figured things at the law firm would slow down until after the New Year.

There was very little evidence that it was close to the Christmas holiday on the streets of Philadelphia. Slider figured that it was another sign society was moving away from tradition. He never really celebrated Christmas in the traditional way growing up, a child of the system. The Salvation Army was posted on the occasional street corner ringing the bell for donations. The usual suspects of panhandlers and homeless roamed the streets in the city of brotherly love. A sharp contrast to the business types, shoppers and students moving about the streets in pursuit of whatever. Slider walked down towards city hall blending in and killing time.

Annie's schedule had been hectic but today she figured she would leave just after rush hour, when the PATCO trains were less crowded. She might even get in a little Christmas shopping on her way home from the PATCO station. Slider hung out, had breakfast in a local fast food place and lunch in the city bar. He refrained from drinking, had to be sharp for task at hand. He decided to catch the first rush hour train back to South Jersey and wait it out in the parking lot. He was counting on Annie to wait out the rush hour and arrive on one of the later evening trains. No matter, it would be dark around 4:40, as the calendar closed in on the shortest day of the year, first day of winter.

Chapter Thirty-Two

John Price started working on an idea for another book. It was an idea that he had in the back of his mind for years. He also reached out to a few new agents and had an idea that at least one was going to take a chance on him. He was sure that agents were reluctant to discuss writers for fear of law suits and didn't worry about any stories that Lauren might have passed around about him. He was confident that Lauren would not disclose the background of his book as she was just as likely to suffer at least a minor professional setback if the truth got out.

John continued to search for additional information on the internet about the dead man who had actually written most of his novel. There was nothing to be found other than the obit of Mr. Kname. He read a collection of non-fiction books about Vietnam to see if his name was mentioned again to no avail. He even went as far as attending meetings of a local veterans group to see if anyone knew of him. Nothing. He was sure that if the teacher from Texas had more concrete information that she would have pursued the matter. He also figured that the granddaughter was clueless as to her grandfather's contribution this book, or she would have already been looking for money. It was ironic that she lived only about 40 miles up the road from his house. He didn't dare to try and reach out to her, as he was afraid that she might be able to put two and two together if she knew his real identity. He wondered if she had heard from the school teacher in Texas.

He continued to work on various ideas for a new book while enjoying the benefits of living on the Banana River. The royalties from his best- selling novel continued to roll in and there had even been an offer for him to teach an adult education fiction writing course at a local community college.

Chapter Thirty-Three

Olivia returned from the agility invitational and went back to her routine. Working at the car dealership, occasionally helping her aunt with the boarding kennel and training Steele for agility. She also started training her new addition, a young mixed breed female she called JD. JD was on the soft side temperament wise, but strong and well put together structurally. Olivia had her in a foundation class but she was having trouble especially on the contacts, teeter, dog walk and A frame. Her jumping ability was good and she was fast and seemed to want to work. Olivia figured she was going to take a lot of effort, but the potential seemed to be there.

Steele continued to work hard and his skills improved. The more he ran the better he got. Olivia came to the realization that her life was pretty much defined by her work with the dogs. JD was about 2 inches taller at the withers than Steele and at 55 pounds outweighed him by about 15 pounds. JD was coal black with a few small white markings on her chest. She and Steele and got along well, Steele being aloof and JD laid back. She was one of an abandoned litter of puppies found in a wooded area in Northern Brevard County. The staff at the shelter had named her Jade, but Olivia didn't think it fit her so out of lack for a better name she just shortened it to JD. JD was placed from the shelter but returned by the first home. Olivia, at the urging of her aunt, took the dog in and her veterinarian said she was about a year old. Olivia often wondered why she was returned by the first owner as she was calm, had a stable temperament and seemed very smart.

Olivia continued to struggle with the mystery of her Grandfather's death and continued to question herself for not taking an interest in his murder earlier. The case continued to be classified as an unsolved crime and an occasional phone call to Woodruff did not reveal any new leads. Olivia often thought of moving to Texas. After the will was settled she was the owner of his mortgage free house. The current tenants had been considering a move. The husband's job had relocated in the early fall and the commute was becoming a problem. They said that they would give her ample notice. Olivia would wait and see.

Chapter Thirty-Four

It was about 6:30 and dark, the sleet had started to change over to light snow. The PATCO transit cop was parked along the covered shelter just outside the main doors of the station. The parking lot was divided on each side of the shelter, the pay lots closer to the entrance of the terminal and the free lots further away. Both lots fed into a main access drive. At the end of the drive was a traffic light, the only options were a left hand turn out to a suburban street, or straight that led to two ramps, route 295 north or south. Occasionally someone would park adjacent to the shelter to either pick someone up or drop someone off. The rail line ran from Lindenwold to the east and all the way to 15th street in Philadelphia to the west. Woodcrest Station was approximately one half way from either destination.

The transit cop on duty this night, Sean Prescott, was fairly new. He had taken the job in hopes of getting a vacancy for one of the New Jersey State Police training classes. He was pretty high on the list but figured he had a few years to wait. He was 23 and had 2 years of community college under his belt. He was also in the Air Force reserve, with an MOS of police officer. There was a rash of robberies at several of the PATCO stations so security was increased. One of the incidents, at a station closer to Camden, had resulted in a homicide. Sean watched as the passengers left and entered the station. The parking lots were lit, but the security cameras were not well maintained and it took an act of God to get them repaired. Sean had recently turned three repair orders in for Woodcrest Station. None had been taken care of.

Annie got off the train that arrived at 6:35. She had changed from her heels to slip on rubber boots before she left her office. It was snowing harder now and she pulled a scarf around her neck, buttoned her coat all the way up, clutched her briefcase under her right arm and carried a small package with her left hand. She was parked in the pay lot to the right, three rows back, towards the west side of the lot. The snow started to cover the pavement and walking was slippery. It was easy to spot her as the later trains normally discharged fewer passengers than the rush hour trains. Slider had waited in the rental car parked at the far corner of the west lot in the non-pay area. He approached the station from different angles each time a train discharged passengers. Slider approached the terminal building this time from the west side of the pay lot. He spotted Annie and watched her struggle to keep a foot as she balanced her briefcase and the package she had picked up before leaving the city. The transit cop had started his car and was circling the lot as the passengers spread out walking towards their vehicles in various areas of the parking lot. Slider made his decision, he started down the row of cars traversing in and out in a low crouch, moving towards Annie as she approached her car. His timing was right and he stopped at the front fender of the car next to hers, separated by one space as the car in between had already left the lot.

Annie turned her back as she hit the key fob that unlocked the door, she also hit the remote start button. Slider moved towards her as she bent down to place the briefcase and package in the back seat. In a split second Annie slipped and fell, an act which probably saved her life. Slider fired once and missed, the round shattered the driver's side window of her car. He moved towards her, reached down and grabbed her by the collar of her coat. Annie held on to the car door and swung her free hand towards the gun. It took all of the strength she could muster. Slider's hand was moved slightly and the next round shattered the glass on the driver's side rear door. Particles of glass flew back and struck him in the face and neck. Annie screamed and rolled on her stomach.

Officer Prescott heard the first shot and sped the Ford Explorer towards the west lot. He skidded to a stop three rows in front of Annie's car and exited gun drawn. Slider saw the transit cop's SUV and moved away from Annie and took cover behind another car. He took one more shot, but Annie had rolled closer to her car. He missed, but now he focused on the transit cop who had exited the SUV. Sean called out identifying himself and instructed Slider to drop his weapon. Slider fired between two cars and Sean fired back over Slider's head. Slider was bleeding from the broken glass and decided to run for it. Sean moved towards Annie and called for backup. He couldn't see Slider well enough to take another shot. It was snowing harder now and the visibility was deteriorating. A few riders heading towards their cars ducked to avoid the gunfire. Slider figured that other police would be on the way and left the rental. He ran towards the tree lined embankment bordering route 295. The embankment was steep and the footing poor, had it not been for the abundance of evergreen trees on the slope Slider would have never made it to the top. Using the evergreen trees for balance and grip he climbed up towards the guardrail separating the highway from the station. The branches produced more scratches on his already bleeding face. The parking lot lighting didn't extend to the embankment, therefore it was impossible to see him climbing up towards 295. He was able to scale the embankment unnoticed. When he got to the top he scaled the guardrail, crossed the three northbound lanes in heavy traffic, scaled the median guardrail and crossed the southbound lanes. He reached the guardrail on the other side and disappeared into the night.

Chapter Thirty-Five

Annie was transported to a local hospital and was treated for scratches, bruises and had small shards of glass removed from her face and hands. Her injuries were dressed and she was kept overnight for observation. She was lucky as there were no serious injuries other than the trauma from the incident.

The crime scene was taped off as the investigators attempted to interview any witnesses who remained. Most of the few who were in the parking lot during the altercation left, to avoid getting involved. The few that volunteered to stay could not provide any details. Most were in survival mode when the shooting started and were face down in the parking lot. There was no trace of the suspect. Annie was interviewed twice within the next two days and was unable to provide any description or details. She had no idea why this happened to her and the original thought about motive was robbery.

The local news stations picked up on the story the next day but details were sparse. The Philadelphia Inquirer missed the Tuesday edition because of the publishing deadline but buried a 10 line article on the incident in the Wednesday South Jersey metro section. No mention was made of the trial Annie was working on. The article ended with a statement asking to call the listed numbers of the local police with any information about the shooting.

Slider knew in his heart that he had messed up, his career was over and his life was in jeopardy. He resigned himself to the fact that he was going to spend the rest of his life looking over his shoulder. His first order of business was to get out of the Philadelphia area. There were two calls to police regarding a suspicious looking man in two separate neighborhoods along the PATCO line. Police that responded didn't find anyone on the streets fitting the descriptions. Just before midnight Slider boarded PATCO at the Fernwood station on the last train to Philadelphia on Monday. He exited at Market street East. The train was occupied by very few passengers and nobody noticed the cuts on his face or the torn and blood stained jacket. Slider was too late for the last train from Market Street to the airport, the R-2 line, so he slipped into one of the local late night shot and beer bars and ordered a sandwich and nursed a few draft beers. The bar was not crowded and nobody noticed or engaged him.

He cleaned up the best he could in the dirty, space limited men's room in the bar. He ditched the denim jacket in a dumpster outside the bar. On his way out of the bar he took a wool pea coat that was left by a customer on the back of bar stool. After closing he left and wandered the streets near Market Street station. He fit in perfectly with the occasional homeless person out on the streets of the city of brotherly love. He caught the first early morning R-2 line to the Philadelphia airport.

Chapter Thirty-Six

Over the years Slider had prepared for a situation that he was sure he would face at some time in his line of work. Because of the nature of his job befriending co-workers was frowned upon so he was on his own. Obtaining alternative identities was easier than one might imagine but it was costly. Rather than just rely on one, he did two. These were in addition to the various identities given to him by his employer. He managed his finances well and took advantage of the liberal expense policy provided by the job. He set up accounts under both IDs and had sufficient amounts of funds in on line banks. Included were credit cards, lines of credit, which he never used, and two safe addresses complete with PO boxes and safe deposit boxes in two different banks. Occasionally he would deposit cash in the safe deposit boxes. He also managed to obtain driver's licenses, passports and cell phone numbers under the two identities. Expensive, yes, necessary yes, especially now.

Slider now knew he would spend the rest of his life on the run. He also knew that any employment in the future would be under the table low profile jobs. Although he would spend the rest of his life looking over his shoulder, he looked forward to be out of the "business."

Late on that Tuesday morning in December Slider boarded an American Airlines flight from Philadelphia to Pittsburgh. He was surprised at how easily he got through the TSA inspectors at Philadelphia. Even the with the coat he grabbed at the bar he still looked and smelled as though he were a homeless person. He just made the flight to Pittsburgh but he had a three hour layover there before he could catch a connecting flight to Denver. During the three hour layover in Pittsburgh Slider purchased clothing and a small duffle bag at the airport mall. He got cleaned up in one of the airport bathrooms and tried to hide the bruises on his face as best as possible. He was pretty sure there would be permanent scars on his face, which might be a good thing considering his situation. Two of the "scratches" were actually lacerations but he was able to get the bleeding to stop. They were noticeable but didn't illicit any response from other passengers. The early morning flight from Philadelphia to Pittsburgh was only about half full. Slider's new life had started. He was sure that the word on him had already been distributed by his now former employer. After the three hour wait he caught the flight from Pittsburgh to Denver.

Chapter Thirty-Seven

In early January 2018 Olivia made the decision. The family renting her Grandfather's house contacted her and said that the commute for the husband from Pilot Point to Decatur was taking a toll and requested to break the lease and move by March 1st. Olivia granted their request. She contacted the property management company located in Denton to inspect the house and inform her of any immediate issues to be taken care of for occupancy. She also informed them that she would be living in the home sometime after March 1st.

She started the process of packing, deciding what she needed and what she didn't and decided that other than her two dogs, almost everything else was disposable. Aunt Kim wasn't surprised and indicated that she figured sooner or later Olivia would leave Florida. She said that she never expected that Texas would be her choice of destinations. Her employer didn't comment one way or the other but even she had to admit that they had treated her fairly, even though she was only a part timer.

As it turned out the Texas property was well taken care of only needing a few minor repairs. The property management company hired a handyman, had a cleaning service spruce the place up a bit, trimmed and cleaned up a few areas on the land. Arrangements were made to turn on the utilities after the tenants left, and Olivia purchased a bedroom set, part of a living room set and a small kitchen table and chairs on line through a local furniture outlet. The property management company provided an employee to supervise the delivery. Olivia was relieved that the only things she had to take would fit in the Toyota FJ.

Kimberly was ok with the move, and stated that she felt Olivia was making a sound decision. She and Olivia met for lunch in early March 2018 at a small restaurant in an old mall located in Titusville. The mall had mostly vacant store sites but the little Italian place did a booming business in both takeout and sit down lunches and dinners. The dress was casual, the service and food great and the fare modest.

Kim was dressed in sweats and a light jacket, as the weather was on the cool side. Olivia had on denim shorts, a navy blue hoodie and running shoes.

"No drama here Kim, no tears you will be able to find extra kennel help when you hit the road for more shows," Olivia smiled and winked, letting her know it was all in jest.

"You know your agility career will suffer, I hear that there are not many trials out there and the travel between venues is a load." Kim smiled back and then continued, "I never considered that you might end up living in your grandfather's home. You should take advantage of what he left you and seize the opportunity to move on with your life. Remember, change is good, and you are still young."

"I can't really say why I am doing this, I don't even know where I will get a job, or whatever, but he left me in a pretty good situation money wise."

"You're not going to play detective on me now, are you," Kim asked.

"What do you mean, I don't understand."

Kim leaned forward and almost whispered, "You have been fighting the circumstances around his murder for a few years now, you should give it up. He really never did much for you or anyone other than himself. He really wasn't much of a support for your mom. I didn't dislike him, he stepped up after I took you, there was never any issues regarding support. It's just that he seemed to me to be self-centered. Like it was all about him. Remember they say everything points to a professional hit, so what's the point."

"I don't know, I can't get it out of my mind, you know, what could he have been involved in that would make someone kill him."

Kim shrugged moved back, and then leaned across the table again, "you ever hear from that friend of his, the one who lives in Oklahoma?"

"You mean Spader, I leave him messages all the time, even e mail requests for just conversation. He never responds, but the detective who I talked to said he probably wouldn't answer anything unless in person."

"Sounds like another self- centered asshole to me. You know it is pretty much what I have seen with Vietnam vets. They were like the throwaways of society, then the ones who made it out of that place, they just turn away from everyone. It's like fuck you, I quit."

Olivia leaned back and shook her head from side to side of, "I don't know, never really thought about Vietnam until he got killed. You know they don't even teach it in school, I never had it in history class. Like, shit it never even existed."

"There was a dog handler quite a few years back, when I was apprenticing with that shithead Bernard, can't remember his name. He was a Vietnam vet, walked with a limp, never asked him why. Anyway, he was quiet, always dressed in second hand store jackets and ties. Sometimes he looked like he was hung over. He was a good handler though, had a real nice touch with a dog. Even with the limp, he could move a dog around the ring. Was really better than most of the other handlers, just sort of didn't fit in. Handled mostly working group breeds. Anyway, he sort of disappeared and later I heard he died of a drug overdose. I often wondered about him, he was always pleasant, good to the dogs, which is the most important thing. He always seemed distant. I guess the war got the best of him."

"That's sad, how well did you know him."

"Not well, but he just seemed like such a nice guy, never made excuses, you know, took the wins and losses the same. Never lost his temper, never gossiped about others. Bernard asked him one time to cover a dog, Bernard had a few conflicts, I took one, Mike, I think that was his name took the other. He took the breed with the dog, I covered the dog in the group. By the way, did the detective or the PI guy think that Spader might have any info, or leads."

"Not really, I just thought that any ideas about that they were keeping to himself, um I mean themselves. Like everything else about it, a mystery."

Kim ordered her meal from the waitress and waited for Olivia to complete her order before continuing.

"Do you think it has anything to do with Vietnam, his murder."

"No, like I told you about what the detective said, why would they wait all these years to kill him?"

"I don't know, maybe we should change the subject, and by the way when you get settled you need to find yourself a cowboy, you are way too pretty to sleep alone."

"Kim, right now I got my dogs, and I got an adventure ahead of me, I'll think about stuff as it comes, won't set myself up for disappointment. Anyway, I suppose Texas has more to offer than just cowboys."

Kim and Olivia ate, talked about dogs and competing and when she left Olivia was confident that she had both Kim's blessing and support regarding her move.

Chapter Thirty-Eight

The far North Texas climate pleased Olivia. There are four distinct seasons, the winters are not as cold as the northern most states and the summers, although hot, were not as humid as Florida. Neighbors were few but friendly on the road where the house, now her house, was located. She knew that her grandfather would live in an area where he was somewhat isolated. The house was well maintained, thanks to the renters that cared and a good property management company. Adjusting and getting settled took longer than she expected. Things like locating a good veterinarian, banking services, driver's license, car registration and finding her way around were high priorities. Even with cellphone directions she liked to know how to get places without relying on google maps. She also had to start a job search, she wasn't really sure what she wanted to do but it seemed as though the job market in the area was strong. She purchased furniture at local stores and decorated the house with western motif located at local flea markets.

She put training her dogs on hold for a while and realized that it was a fact that there were few facilities for trials close by. She eventually found a trainer who had good equipment, a well maintained training building and the lessons were reasonably priced. Steele took the move in stride but her rescue JD struggled with the new surroundings. The house sat on a little over 4 acres of ground with an area off the back porch securely fenced with ample room for the dogs to get exercise.

The property included a large steel garage / storage building which contained all of the equipment that her grandfather used to maintain the property. She was going to have to learn to use the John Deere zero turn mower and other outdoor equipment. Hard work, especially outdoors, didn't intimidate her.

Major shopping meant a little drive, either Denton to the south or Gainesville or Sherman to the north. The immediate area had a few small family owned grocery stores and an abundance of convenience stores coupled with gas stations. She really liked the locals, they were friendly and very helpful. She eventually found a part time job working in a local store that sold everything from western wear and feed supplies to outdoor equipment. It was family owned and had three locations, two in Grayson county and one in Denton county. Her hours were fairly steady and they were closed on Sunday's, which would allow her to resume running the dogs when she could get back in the routine.

Chapter Thirty-Nine

After her initial settling in process she had two priorities. One was contacting and meeting Eddie Spader and the other was contacting and meeting with Linda Rossi. She figured that Spader was the top priority, both lived close. Rossi lived the closest to her grandfather's now her home and Spader in Southern Oklahoma. She figured that Spader was only about 35 or 40 miles from her. She e-mailed both and also left a message on Spader's voice mail. Much to her surprise Spader answered with a phone call and offered to meet anywhere she wanted on her terms. It was already the middle of May 2018 and she figured that since part of the reason she moved was to try and find out more about her grandfather's death she might as well move on it. She and Spader played phone tag for a few weeks while she cleared up a day or two off from her job. She agreed to come to his home and he offered an early afternoon visit so she would be comfortable and have time to get back home as she was still getting used to driving in the area. They agreed on a date early in June. Olivia found that she wasn't intimidated and looked forward to the meeting. Although her contact with her grandfather was limited and sporadic he always spoke very highly of Eddie Spader. She was also able to reach Linda Rossi and they were able to set up a meeting for lunch the next week. As it turned out Rossi lived only about a 20 minute drive from Olivia's home. They met in a small restaurant in nearby Whitesboro.

Chapter Forty

Linda Rossi arrived first, took a seat at a table. She smiled and stood up and greeted Olivia. Linda looked much younger than her age, 59. She was dressed in shorts, a plain white t shirt and flip flops. She was barely 5′4″ and looked up at the taller Olivia. Her grey streaked blond hair was long and she pulled it back in a ponytail. Olivia dressed down but had already acquired a taste for Southwestern apparel. She sported a short jeans skirt and a plaid snap buttoned western shirt. She usually covered her hair with a baseball cap and this one advertised a Texas brand of outdoor apparel. After preliminary exchanges Linda started the conversation.

"First, your grandfather and I were more than just friends. We were involved, both physically and emotionally on more than a casual level."

"You mean you were sleeping with him."

Linda laughed, and replied, "Yeah, I really liked him, even the age difference, 12 years, didn't bother me. I have never been married and I wasn't looking for that, I just fell for him."

Olivia smiled, shook her head and replied, "hey it's ok, my grandmother and him divorced years ago, way before I was even born, I'm just happy that he had the relationship."

"I never pressed him, I knew from the get go that it would end at some point, nothing permanent, but I never dreamed he would be killed."

"Were you still involved when he went to Florida?"

"Yeah, for sure. When he bought the motor home he said he wanted to travel round a bit, so figured it was a signal, like he was done with me. But you know, he and I used it a lot. We went down to the Gulf Coast a few times and fished. He showed me all about it, fishing, I learned to bait the hook, cast and just enjoy nature. He bought me a fancy surf reel and a 10 foot long surf pole, I still have it. I have never used it since he died but would never part with it. He would take me fishing, we would come back, shower, sometimes together, that is really hard in an RV shower stall, but it worked. Have a few drinks, beers, and then we would catch a baseball game on the satellite dish. They were some of the best times of my life."

Olivia stopped her, and asked, "why did he go Florida without you?"

"We talked about it, he said he wanted to see you and his niece, he wanted to spend some time alone, but he kept in touch, and we parted on what I thought was good ground. I didn't think anything about it. He even talked about me seeing you and Kim, his niece, sometime, like on another trip. He said Kim raised you right."

"Yeah, she did, we are close, sometimes I think it was an imposition on her life style but she was good to me. Can you remember the last time you had contact?"

"I had not heard from him for about a week, but that wasn't unusual. He would text a few days and then skip a few days, sometimes he would call or e mail. When I saw the obit I was devastated."

"The others in your group, did they know about your relationship with my grandfather?"

Linda paused, before answering. "I'm not sure, we didn't advertise, I always respected what I thought was his desire for privacy. I didn't matter to me if people knew, I just never really talked to him about it."

"Any ideas why someone would kill him, and do you think that the writing had anything to do with it."

"No idea at all, he rarely spoke about Vietnam, his job afterwards and always referred to the part time thing with the detective agency as penny ante bullshit. Those were his exact words. I think it was one of his favorite terms."

Olivia was curious and got to the big question, "what about the book that guy wrote."

"You know Olivia, I read a lot of books about Vietnam, I told you my neighbor's son died over there, I still remember his parents grief, how they mourned for years, he was their only son. I was only about 6 or 7 but I remember him, he was a quiet kid, always smiling, never heard a bad word out of his mouth. He was only 18, he died about three months after he left. I can remember how bitter his family was over that war. Sorry, I probably told you this on the phone, you get older you repeat stuff a lot. I have digressed here."

"No it's ok, keep talking." Olivia interrupted.

"Anyway, when I read the Price book, I saw so many similarities to something your grandfather was working on. Started asking questions but the others in the group didn't express an opinion. Maybe they knew I was involved more than casually and felt I was looking too hard at it."

"Do you think it is worth pursuing, and do you think it had anything to do with his murder?"

"No, on either count, my brother's current girlfriend is a lawyer, or at least she claims to be, personally I don't know how she got through law school, but that is another story. Anyway she said that pursuing it was a stretch, especially since there was no copy of his writings. I would guess that it was on his laptop, but who knows where that ended up."

Olivia thought for a moment about the laptop, how it was missing from the evidence locker, then she changed the subject, "Linda, did you ever meet Eddie Spader, or did my grandfather ever mention him."

"I never met him, Rick talked about him all the time, he also talked about Clifford. I know that he occasionally saw Spader and I'm sure that they had a few drinks with each other from time to time. The man I knew, was in my opinion, almost flawless, if there was another side to him, I didn't know it. I'm sure Spader, based on his conversations about him, knows that side if it exists. I'll never understand why he was killed."

Olivia and Linda shared a few other things with each other, none having to do with Rick Kname. Linda gave her some tips on living in North Texas, her survival guide to the southwest. After a long leisurely lunch they parted ways but agreed to meet from time to time and remain in touch. On the way home Olivia thought about the Linda's comment about the laptop. Olivia wondered if the laptop had anything to do with her grandfather's murder. It was clearly stated in the police report that the laptop was in plain view on the small kitchen table just to the left of the entrance to the RV. She figured that the investigation didn't consider the laptop because it wasn't taken during the "commission of the crime," words verbatim from the report. She wasn't even sure if the subject of Price and the book were ever considered by Woodruff, but then again the book was published two years after the murder.

Chapter Forty-One

Jake's campground, located in the southwest corner of Arkansas below Lewisville, is a family owned business. Lonnie runs the place for his uncle. In addition to RV facilities the camp ground has a dozen cabins that are rented for either short or long term occupancy. Tenants aren't screened and cash payments are preferred. Lonnie knows that occasionally he might rent to someone on the run for one reason or another. In the past the local sheriff's office or state police occasionally came out looking for fugitives. Lonnie always cooperated and there was never any serious issues. As long as law enforcement wasn't knocking on the door, Lonnie minded his own business even when he suspected someone was renting for more than just getting away from it all.

On this early June morning two large men entered the office, dressed in suits, out of character for the area. Lonnie noticed that they parked a black suburban outside the office. Lonnie, no light weight himself, pushed his way by and checked out the SUV and noted that it had Florida plates. Probably a rental. The two men were both well over 6 foot and easily north of 225 pounds.

"Can I help you?"

The taller of the two placed a photo of a man on the counter and a 50 dollar bill on top of the counter. Lonnie looked at the photo, it was the clean shaven version of a man who rented a cabin from early January to just before Memorial Day. The man had registered under what Lonnie figured was an alias and drove an old Jeep CJ with Colorado plates. Lonnie never bothered to check the registration as the man paid month to month cash in advance. He was quiet, polite and minded his own business. Just before leaving he thanked Lonnie, squared his bill and tipped Lonnie a 100 dollar bill, and a case of Budweiser. Lonnie shook his hand and noted that he had grown a full beard. He appeared to be around 40 or so, average height, in pretty good shape with thinning blond hair that he always covered with a baseball cap.

"And," Lonnie commented after glancing at the photo.

"Listen man, you seen this guy, before you lie to me, he has been seen in this area, we have what they call credible evidence to that fact."

"I don't know what credible means," Lonnie knew he was bluffing because the locals wouldn't talk to these two let alone give them any information. They both flashed badges, which Lonnie also knew was a bluff because they didn't allow him to inspect. One of them pushed his suit jacket back far enough to reveal what looked like a Glock pistol holstered on his right hip.

Lonnie smiled and reached below the counter and produced a Smith and Wesson 357 magnum with a 6 inch barrel. "I got my own here, you see, maybe we need to call the local sheriff just to see if that gun is legal."

The other man started to lean over the counter and Lonnie stuck the business end of the revolver in his chest.

"I wouldn't if I were you, this ain't Florida and here in Arkansas I got legal grounds to blow both of you away.

"Fuck you asshole, we know this guy was here, so you better fess up, and you better get that six shooter out of my chest."

Lonnie pressed the gun harder and pulled back the hammer, "may be a six shooter but it will only take me two to take both you fat assholes out, and that leaves 5 more in the chambers. By the way, they are 7 shooters nowadays, you are both dead before you get that plastic gun out of your holster. Is my math right, dickhead, you know 2 minus 7, leaves 5, right"?

The other man started to move himself to the right, like he was looking for distance. Lonnie eased back from the counter so as not to give them an advantage, he figured the other guy was armed also. Neither man noticed the door, but Lonnie smiled, he nodded and both guys looked back at the door. Unbeknownst to both of them Lonnie's little brother was standing in the doorway. Allen worked part time at the campground and had just happened to the office when the two thugs came inside. Not liking the looks of either one, he went back to his pickup truck and retrieved his trusty 12 gauge Winchester shotgun.

Now in a potential crossfire, both men shyly walked backwards towards the door. Allen stepped aside and allowed them passage to the parking lot.

The taller one spoke as they exited," we'll be back asshole, you can bet on it."

Allen countered with," ok, come on back down. I would like nothing better than to blow your pea brain out of your ugly face."

Lonnie tucked the 50 in his wallet, threw one 20 on the counter, pointed to them and told Allen, "take your cut man."

Allen smiled, "hey I seen them two, not liking the looks of either I figured you might need a hand."

Lonnie replied, "yeah, I guess they figured we don't have guns, but I was ok, but with you in the door they was in a crossfire, that really scared the shit out of them."

"What did they want, do you think they is coming back."

"Remember the guy who stayed in the cabin, the end one closest to the lake. They had a picture of him, said they was looking for him, and no I don't think they will be back."

"Think he is in trouble, the guy who rented the cabin?"

"I don't know and I don't care. Now get back to work, and thanks, that Winchester has a way of convincing people, especially assholes like those two."

Lonnie figured that whatever the renter had done, he was certainly wanted but not by the cops.

Chapter Forty-Two

Olivia finally confirmed the arrangement and headed up to Spader's home in Oklahoma. She had no trouble finding his place and when she pulled in Franklin "Eddie" Spader was sitting outside at a small picnic table smoking a cigarette. He looked his age, had his thick, long gray hair pulled back in a ponytail and sported a pair of Oakley shades. His well- worn Dickies work pants were cutoff at the knees and a cutoff gray pocket t shirt displayed numerous tattoos on his arms. She noted that his arms were muscular and sort of offset what looked like an ample midsection, but not enough to be called fat. Maybe just heavy set. It was warm but overcast and not uncomfortable to be outside. Olivia had green cargo shorts and an Adidas t shirt in off white, flip flops and a Dallas Stars baseball cap. She moved from the FJ, Spader stood up and extended his hand, they shook and he asked he her to sit down. She nodded and complied.

"I am going to have a beer, you want anything, before we get started. I always pictured you as you look, Rick told me that you got the good family genes and he described you perfectly."

"I'll have a drink, anything domestic will do, just one, I am still getting used to the area and although it was easy to find you, it was a little further, or maybe just a little longer of a drive than I thought."

Spader went in the house and returned with two bottles of Budweiser. While he was in the house Olivia noticed that the house and surrounding property were very well maintained. She noted the Toyota pickup truck and it too, although dated was very clean and looked in almost factory new condition. The rear window had an NRA decal and the bumper an Oklahoma University bumper sticker.

Spader started, "Were do you want to start, I don't figure you came here to hear me talk about myself, and I'm sure you don't want to talk about yourself. That only leaves your grandfather, Rick, so I guess that's what you want, or where you want me to start."

"I'm not sure, I guess there are so many questions, things I am curious about. I didn't take notes, and I am sure you can't cover everything, or maybe you don't want to."

"Don't worry Olivia, don't make yourself a stranger, we can take it in bits, I guess the main thing on your mind is what I know, or what you think I know about his death."

"Yeah, I guess, but I talked to the police, I talked to the guy Vanderkelen, I read the reports and mostly got very little out of anything. The big thing is that I waited all this time, I can't help but have some guilt, but then again he wasn't really involved much in my life, and yet he did pay all the bills on my, I can't think of the word, should I say upbringing."

"Olivia, Rick also felt guilt. He was a restless soul, always looking for the next adventure. Unfortunately that may have been his undoing, somewhere along the line he stepped on the wrong something or other, and he was killed for it."

"How did he end up in Texas, I know he lived here for quite a few years, but it didn't seem to fit, after all he grew up in Ohio."

"When he worked for Pacific Engineering they sent him down here a lot and he liked the state, especially in the northern part, north of what they call the DFW metroplex."

"What did he do for them, what were they?"

Spader smiled and took a swig of his beer, "nothing more than a contractor for the military. Nothing cloak and dagger, just simple shit, you know, I can't think of the right way to describe them. Gofers, I guess, overflow of stuff the military didn't have the time or manpower to take care of. Like if there was an AWOL guy that they had a lot of bad leads on, they might check some of the leads out. Never got involved in any stuff where the guy, or girl now that the military has a lot of women in, were accused of violent stuff. Might say they were sort of, but not actually, bounty hunters. The government employs a lot of people who do stuff you never read about, but not anything that serious or anything classified, just as Rick used to say penny ante bullshit."

"So that had nothing to do with his being killed, right?"

"Yeah," Spader lit another cigarette. "Rick, he got bored with it, he never had much for authority, and his last boss there was, in his words, a guy that would step on you first before throwing you under the bus. He was there for almost 10 years, most of it in Texas and Oklahoma. It was good for us, we got to see a lot of each other. He was without a doubt the best friend I ever had."

"Do you know anything about, like why or who killed him, did you tell the detective and Vanderkelen everything you knew."

"Look, I can only guess, but in my opinion the locals left a lot unlooked at. Vanderkelen seemed pretty sharp, but he had issues with the locals, it was pretty well known, his stuff. They really made him eat a lot of shit, you know. But as they say, at the end of the day it don't matter, it was a professional hit and if the guy is still working or even living, I'd be surprised. My guess is that they replace those types regularly and they don't let them live once they are done with them."

"So you think whoever did it is dead."

"I don't know, I just figure they don't last real long doing that for a living."

"Could it have been random."

"No way, there was a reason, from what the detective, what's his name."

"Woodruff."

"Yeah right, all the stuff left right there, the money, couple of guns, you know other stuff, it was a hit."

"How about a mistake, maybe meant for someone else."

Spader hesitated, "you know that was never even mentioned to me by either Woodruff, or Vanderkelen, I never really thought about it. You know, when they call for hits you think they must spend time looking at the person, looking for the person. Then I think they would watch him, or her, for at least a few days, looking at habits, stuff like that. But it is an interesting thought. Even though they never said anything about it, I'm sure they must have it least thought it. But how far are they going to take it, you know from what they say no clues, messed up crime scene you know all that."

Olivia examined the level in the beer bottle, "do you think it had anything to do with Vietnam, anything he did over there?"

"Hell no, if it did me and Clifford would be dead by now anyway. Without talkin a lot about that place, do you know what he did over there?"

"No, he never, ever talked about it, to me or to Kim, she is his niece, she raised me after my mom died."

"I know the story, me and Rick talked about it all, I know the history. Your aunt and stuff. Most guys don't talk about it much, Vietnam, there is a saying, you wouldn't believe the things that went on over there. That's the best way to put it."

Chapter Forty-Three

Eddie stopped the conversation at that point and suggested he make them something to eat. Olivia agreed and he went inside and heated up some brisket he had smoked and made sandwiches served with fresh spinach and he talked her into another beer. Olivia liked his house, the furniture and other items were all old looking, and with a definite southwest theme. The paintings were in what looked like home- made frames fashioned from timber that at one time might have been parts of an old barn. She could tell that he put a lot of work into it. They also discussed Linda Rossi and the book that was written by John Price. She was surprised that he had read the book but disappointed when he called it fiction. He qualified his statement by saying that all fiction has some basis in fact, but since he had not read any of Rick's stuff he couldn't comment on any similarities between the book and Rick's experiences. He commented "that a lot of stuff has been written about Vietnam, so anyone could read stuff and then write stuff based on what they read. " Back outside Spader continued the conversation getting back to Olivia's grandfather.

"Like I said do you have any idea what he did over there? I guess the time has come for me to tell you. It was no big secret, the shit we did, more than the government wanted people to know. I guess a little history lesson would help with this stuff."

"Not my strong point in school, history."

"You see sometime in 1968 or 69 the brass decided to go to another way in the war. There was a lot of protests and all at home, and an election, new president, changes in what they called the mission. So they decided to start trying to talk the village and hamlet chiefs into taking our side, you know, be a democracy. But the NVA and VC were working them from the other side. Some of the hamlet and village chiefs would, as you say, play both ends against the middle. You know, I'll take from you and I'll take from them. Well when these chiefs were double crossing us instead of trying to make them change they decided to just kill them. Call them double agents, make it look like a James Bond thing, no that's not right, forget that I never liked that James Bond shit anyway. So, that's what we did, your grandfather, me and Clifford. We were a team, Rick, your grandfather was, I guess you could say an assassin. See where it fits in, with the book that that guy wrote."

"How did my grandfather end up doing that, I don't see where that could happen."

"Like I said, you wouldn't believe the things that went on over there. The intelligence guys were all officers, some spoke Vietnamese, it made sense. But you see, Rick spoke Vietnamese, the hard way."

"What, I don't get it", Olivia half smiled and half frowned.

"When Rick enlisted they tested him, like everyone, even the draftees, you had to take a test. Most guys were just passed off as grunts, you know infantry. They saw where he had an ability to learn languages and they sent him to a quickie language school. I think they really wanted him to be an officer, but he didn't like the authority and the rules. So they made him an infantryman."

Olivia interrupted, "how did you get pulled in with him, and Clifford too, where did he fit in?"

"Rick was a natural, his first tour he was in an infantry platoon, a squad leader. They were in the shit. So they figured with his combat experience, his Vietnamese, you know speaking it and understanding what they say, he was a natural. You know his Vietnamese was pretty good, he could go beyond the basics. Sometimes I was like blown away, you could tell the Vietnamese, the villagers, were like, hey, he understands, we can't bullshit this guy."

"I still don't figure where you two got in."

"I was driving for a Colonel, easy duty, but too much stateside routine. Rick and me talked a lot, and he asked me to join him. He was upfront, you know you could get killed and all that, but I took it, thought it might not be all that bad. Clifford was the radio operator in Rick's platoon. Rick liked him, he was quiet, and very calm, even in tight spots, and he was willing. He didn't get along with the CO, so he figured it was a way out of the CO's sight."

"Were you ok, what did you think about the killing."

"It was a war, that's what people do, they kill. Your grandfather never asked us to do his job. I never thought much about it. We would find the guy, make sure it was the right guy and Rick would do the job, off him. Me and Clifford would watch out, get us in and out of the area, backup your grandfather when needed. Most of the time it went, I guess you could say easy. If you can say killing is easy. We had a few close calls, but we managed. The drop offs and pickups were always pretty much on time. It wasn't like recon, you know out there on your own for days, sometimes weeks at a time. Don't know that I could get with that. They never let us hang, the intelligence guys, officers planned it out real well. Sometimes we went as much as a month between jobs, and most of the time the intelligence was right, the guy was usually where he was supposed to be. We always had pictures and shit to ID him. It was also an example to others, you know the next chief, like if you screw us, we will get you."

"That's what he did, you did."

"I wasn't the trigger man, your grandfather was. But you know I ended up with a friend for life. Don't think he was a bad guy, he did his job, he carried out his orders, and in the end taking these guys out probably saved the lives of our guys. A lot of our guys. Figure most of our guys didn't want to be there, but they as they say now manned up. You know the bad village chiefs were double crossing, giving us bad information, causing our guys to get killed."

"I have a big question," Olivia took a breath and sat forward on the bench, "what did he think about the war, or you or Clifford, I said they never taught us anything in school, like it never happened. I would say to someone in school or a friend, hey my grandfather was in Vietnam, they would say, like and, what's your point. Was it patriotic?"

Spader laughed and took a big gulp of Budweiser, then lit a cigarette. "All three of us enlisted, most of the guys were draftees, it's like today, they call it the all-volunteer Army, or military, whatever. So today if you fuck up or complain they say, hey you signed up for this shit, it's your fucking job. But back then they needed a purpose, so they told everyone it was about communism. If you don't stop it here, in Vietnam, they will be in your back yard. They called it the domino theory."

Olivia started to interrupt, but Spader put his hand up to stop her.

"It was the start of what is going on today, maybe even before Vietnam, like Korea, but I don't know shit about Korea. We have troops everywhere, its stopping terrorism, going after this bad leader, or that bad leader, always an excuse. Rick saw through it, back then, all the way until he died. He was so smart. I don't know exactly where it started with him, but he got there. Vietnam was about money, really, lot a fat cats got rich over it. Lotta fat asshole politicians too, ever wonder how politicians get rich. They stick their hands in someone else's pocket. That's how."

Olivia got a quick word in, "what about you, what do you think."

"Listen, I'm not done on Rick. Also the French were there before us, they had a lot at stake when they got run out. We protected stuff for them, do you know how many rubber tree plantations are over there. Can you say Michelin. They are making money over there. People in the country, Vietnam, in this country are making money, everybody gettin rich, you know. Well except for the Vietnamese regular people, farmers you know. Rick used to say that place smelled of money. Another thing, ever see the list of politicians and celebrities that avoided the draft, it's like a who's who list. Rick always said that it was a shame, young men, going over there, die for nothing, so some asshole could get rich. The politicians and the rich assholes got their hand in everybody's pocket, on the take. Ever wonder how many of their kids was over there? None, it was the guy working in a steel mill, auto factory or some contractor, average working people, the poor, it was their kids, the ones dying, no problem for the politicians or asshole business men."

Spader paused, took another swig from the Bud, put out the cigarette in an ash tray that looked like it was 100 years old.

"That's how he saw it. You know, they were running short on bodies, who wanted to go over there, all kinds of ways to get out of it, money, college boys, draft dodgers, you know. So the secretary of defense, can't think of his name, he lowered the standards on draftees and guys enlisting. The test scores, they could be lower. Rick used to say that many of them shouldn't be in the army, let alone in a war. One time he tells me, hey on my first tour we had this kid in my squad, he was slow, real slow. We set up an ambush, I tell the kid take a claymore out and set it up on the perimeter. The claymore is an anti- personnel mine, it is small, is connected by a wire to a hand held charging device. Well it says on the mine, this side towards enemy. Well Rick goes out to check it and the kid had it pointing back to the guys set up on the ambush. Rick turns it around the right way, comes back, but instead of giving the kid shit, he talks to him. The kid tells him, hey I can't read, I never even got past the 5th grade. Go figure."

Olivia tries to interject, Spader puts his hand up, lights another cigarette.

"Like I said he was smart, I think he was able to figure out from his contact with the officers, from intelligence, see through the bullshit they were talking."

"You and Clifford, how about you two."

"Clifford was a shy kid, he joined probably because he had nothing else to do, he did his job, we liked him, calm, easy going, dependable. Not sure about his views, he never talked much about stuff, kept to himself. Me, Rick sort of rubbed off on me. He would say, hey look at this shit, what's this shit all about. He liked the word shit. Also all the lives we wasted, and the money. Rick would say hey, they don't want this to end, the fat cats in Washington are lining their pockets, he always used that saying, term. He always talked about the money, today they call it following the money. I'm about winded here, but you know after a while I started to look at it a different way, and guess what, he was right."

Olivia started to say something then Spader stopped her again.

"Last point, we all hated draft dodgers, all of us, Rick called them the phony baloneys. But he said something to me one of the last times I saw him, and I can't get it out of my mind. He used to say I wonder what the draft dodgers are going to tell their grandchildren. Then he hits me with this, you now Spade, that's what he called me, never Franklin, never Eddie, never Spader, just Spade. They don't teach history, they want to change history today, I figured it's because they don't have to make an excuse to their grandchildren. Tell them their grandfather was a coward while others died. Think about it."

Olivia and Spader continued on for a while until she realized she needed to get home and take care of Steele and JD. Olivia wanted to know about the job with the PI agency, and Spader said he would come down to her place and they could talk about it. He also told her that Rick had a storage container rented and it had some personal stuff in it. Spader had the key and the stuff was hers. He said he wasn't sure what was in there, but they could go check it out. It was located south of her near the intersection of 377 and 380.

"Good meeting you, I come down that way from time to time. I see this women, Cristal, we are off and on for about 10 years, the three of us can do a flea market or have a lunch or something if you like. No shop talk around her, this stuff is all personal, I like to leave it that way."

"Sounds good, I'm glad my grandfather had you as a friend, keep in touch, thanks for the brisket and the beers."

On her way home Olivia felt a sense of pride, that her grandfather was unique, and yet humble despite his experiences in what she read was an unpopular time in this country."

Chapter Forty-Four

Olivia continued working and getting used to life in Texas. The summer heat didn't bother her since she had spent most of her life in Florida. The lower humidity made up for the higher temperatures and the hot afternoon sun. She also liked the fact that she lived in the central time zone, even though she didn't watch much TV, the shows or sporting events were all on an hour earlier. She made the house and the property over in her own image, a little at a time.

Steele got back in the training groove and she started JD in what they call ground or basic agility skills class. Even though she was new to the scene in agility circles in North Texas the members of her two classes realized that she was a good handler and adept at moving her dogs along the skill level. The downside was that there were less trials within reasonable driving distances. All trials were indoors and most of the facilities were on dirt surfaces.

Work was a challenge at first but she made a few friends and accepted the advice of co- workers on local issues, such as places to eat, shop and spend free time. It took a while but she was able to make friends with a few neighbors and soon became comfortable. She was confident that the others on the road were of the type that they looked out for each other. She hired help to get the house and property in order and after the visit to Spader's house she was more intent on learning more about her grandfather and his life after the military and work for the government contractor. Although she felt that Spader was forthcoming she had a suspicion that he might have been holding back on a few things. Maybe the contents of container might shed some light on things, only time would tell.

Chapter Forty-Five

Slider knew he would always be on the run. Even with the two clean ID's, money stashed in various accounts under his two names and cash he took the chance to hide in various locations, he knew this would be a challenge. He didn't plan this, but he knew that someday he would have to run from his former employer. He spent hours locating safe places, like the camp ground he stayed at in Arkansas. He had no knowledge of the thugs who came looking for him there, and he was fortunate that the owner and caretakers were "mind your own business types."

His appearance had changed as he snaked his way across the Florida panhandle and down the Gulf Coast working here and there, all cash jobs, no questions asked. He lost some weight, grew a full beard and let his hair grow out. Even though he was thinning on top it grew out fairly full and darker with gray streaks that matched the gray in his beard. The broken glass from the incident in New Jersey had left a few scars on his face and hands. This added to the personal modifications he made to his appearance. He finally landed in early July 2018 between Largo and Clearwater where he took a job at a marina and dry dock yard. The owner was used to temporary help and never asked for ID, SSAN, background or anything much more than a first name. Slider went by the name Troy Cronin and took a rent by the week room in a local motel.

The work was easy and he soon established himself as a reliable, hard working person who asked few questions and minded his own business. Slider's Navy service and mechanical ability had prepared him for a lot of the skills needed to work the marina. The owner was impressed by his skills and work ethic. Slider still had the old Jeep and was able to get away with out of state plates, insurance and driver's license. He drove only when necessary to avoid any problems. The marina was within walking distance of the motel where he stayed. The Jeep had been well maintained and despite being long in tooth was a dependable ride. Transients were common place in Florida and it was one of the reasons he moved in this direction.

Working at the marina exposed him to the sun and he managed to get a nice tan, toned his 40 something body and found that he attracted women in the early 30 to early 40 age range. Most had been married at least once, and he stayed away from any who were recently divorced or ones with kids. He also found a local watering hole called Pete's Grill. Slider knew that his story had to be consistent in order to maintain his anonymity but he had a weakness for telling stories and had to be careful not to get caught in a lie. He also was pining for the affection of a women, and Pete's Grill was a hot spot on some nights.

Chapter Forty-Six

About mid-July Spader came down to Olivia's and they rode out to the storage facility. Spader told her that Rick had left him some money and he rented the storage locker a year at a time and the rent was good until September. He said that prior leaving they would go to the office and make the necessary arrangements to have the locker put in her name. The facility offered three sizes of space, Rick had taken the medium locker, which could hold an ample amount of items.

It was a warm day and the locker was not the high end ones that had climate control. So it was hot inside. The locker was mostly empty, a few pieces of old furniture, two tool boxes and an assortment of fishing equipment. There was also an old metal filing cabinet, with four drawers, three empty and the bottom one had a pad lock on it.

"Don't worry about the lock, a good pair of bolt cutters can take care of that. There is probably a pair in one of those tool boxes. The furniture, well that is probably stuff he had plans to re finish and put in the house. Now, the fishing equipment, he was a fishing expert. I can tell you that it is worth a lot of money, don't let anyone buy it for a song."

Olivia smiled, "Ok so what do I do with it. I can look the stuff up, but then what."

"E bay, newspaper ad, or take some time and rent a table at a flea market and sell it there. Might even try a yard or garage sale. I don't fish, but he often talked about how much he spent on his equipment, and he kept it up. Might even want to keep a few rods and reels, you might catch the fishing bug. The stuff with him in the RV is at my house, you can have that too. We got to talking when you were up there and I forgot about the stuff."

"What about the guns, the detective said he had two in the RV."

"I have them both, they are yours, but if you don't have any experience you should get some lessons. The pistol is a snub nose 38, and there is a 12 gauge shotgun. I could give you a 20 I have in place of the 12, but you have to figure out what you want. The 20 would be easier to handle, less kick, but you make the decision. They are both, the 12 and the 20, Remington 870's. Rick favored US made guns. The snub nose is a Smith and Wesson. His favorite, he used to joke that in a pinch he had two lawyers, Mr. Smith and Mr. Wesson"

Olivia opened the tool boxes and found a small pair of bolt cutters, "will these do."

"Give them to me, that lock will come right off."

Spader cut the lock and pulled the drawer open. Inside were several manila folders with what appeared to be personal papers, some banking receipts and assorted old manuals for various electronic devices and outdoor equipment. There was also a bound folder with no title marked on the outside. Olivia started to page through it and stopped abruptly.

"This looks like some stuff he may have written, I will need to look into it. It is really hot in here so why don't we go back up to the house, I can take these folders with me and go through them later."

"Olivia, if you need help cleaning this place out, I can come down with my truck and help you out. No use renting it past

September, this stuff can be sorted out and stored up at Rick's, I mean your house."

"Thanks, I'll give you a call, I don't need to extend the rent here, nothing else to do. Why do you think he had this, it is hardly one quarter full."

"Rick was a collector, he was always looking for ways to keep busy. He probably intended on restoring the furniture. He really had room for all this stuff at the house. I used to tell him to get another utility building put up, easier and more sense than renting this place. As far as the fishing stuff, he could have stored it in the garage, but he never gave any of it up. I bet some of it is 40 years old."

Spader and Olivia returned to her home. She made a quick lunch, they talked about her grandfather and declined to get into his work at the PI agency on this visit. Spader left and headed up to Oklahoma. After she paged through the documents and writings in the folder she realized that the storage locker held no secrets regarding the murder of her grandfather. She agreed with Spader that keeping it made no sense and she called the manager and told him that it would be cleaned out before September 1 and she would not be renewing the lease.

Chapter Forty-Seven

John Price figured that time had healed the suspicions about his book. Life had gotten better, no more phone calls about the sources of his writing. The part time job at the local Community College worked out well and led him to contacts with a local community newspaper. He wrote several articles for the paper and had done research on issues involving the Merritt Island area. His articles were well received and the fact that he was writing, even though the source was a local paper, took pressure off him to produce a new novel. It was not uncommon for new authors to be "one and done," so he went with it.

The percentage from sales or royalties from the novel, the part time job and the local writing was more than enough to sustain his life style. Plus, he was considered somewhat of a local celebrity. Occasionally getting paid for speaking and promoting local causes. He stayed away as much as possible about conversations regarding Vietnam and it seemed to be working. His new agent was laid back, rarely contacted him and Lauren had long forgotten him. Things had sort of worked out for John Price. He was pretty sure he "was out of the woods" regarding his best- selling novel.

Chapter Forty-Eight

Late July and it was hot and humid in Florida. Slider, or Troy as it was now, showered after work at the marina and headed back to his rented room. Wednesday night and he was feeling pretty good, it had been an easy day at work. He smoked a cigarette and contemplated going to Pete's grill for a sandwich and a couple of cold beers. Usually midweek things were slow and he had no illusions of meeting anyone, but he was suffering from lack of a women. He even figured just conversation with a women would be at least some relief. Flip flops, jean shorts and a clean pocket t shirt covered him, he removed the San Diego Padres baseball cap as he entered and took a stool at the far end of the bar. Pete's oldest son, Pete Jr. was bartending and the TV had a Tampa Bay Ray's pre- game show on. Junior yelled from the far end of the bar, "menu and a cold Bud, right Troy."

"Skip the menu Pete, just give me a grouper sandwich, no fries, and I'll take a shot of Jack with the beer."

"You got it, man."

Slider observed no one else at the bar, but it was only a little after 6, early for any crowd, but Wednesdays were usually slow anyway.

After he finished the sandwich and ordered his second beer, he noticed a women enter the bar, she paused at the row of booths just inside the door and looked towards the bathroom sign. She entered the ladies room.

Pete smiled and looked down the bar at Slider, "Never seen that one Troy, must be a pit stop on her way to a classier joint."

Slider shrugged, "who knows, a little overdressed for your place, but don't put it down, good food, booze and clean bathrooms go long way."

When she came back out she looked down the bar towards Slider and smiled. She had long auburn hair pulled back in a ponytail, tall, dressed in a yellow sundress and expensive looking sandals. She had a pretty smile and very alert brown eyes. She slowly walked down the end of the bar towards Slider.

"You lost, doesn't look like your type of place."

"Are you saving that seat for someone, I can sit at the other end if you like."

Slider motioned for her to sit, she complied and looked down the bar towards Pete Junior.

"How about a vodka martini straight up and cover him for whatever he is drinking."

Slider paused and had to think about what to say, "do I know you, you kind of look out of place, uh I guess I already said that."

She laughed, pulled her sunglasses up on her forehead, smiled again and looked Slider up and down.

"No, but I have seen you, at the marina, friends of mine are docked there temporarily, we had lunch on the boat today, and I saw you laboring in the hot sun. Couldn't help but notice, you look like you know more about boats than the guy who runs the place."

Pete placed the vodka martini in front of the women and an upside down glass in front of Slider.

The women pulled a 50 from her purse and placed it on the bar in front of her drink. Pete took it and walked towards the cash register.

Slider shrugged again, "I don't know, I was in the Navy a long time ago, learned the basics, whatever."

"Ok, let's start, my name is Darla, not on your list of baby names for the year I was born, but I kinda like it, sort of sticks with you, 35 years down the road."

"My name is Troy, cut to the chase, 45 years down the road."

"That was quick, I like that in a man, tell me more, or would you rather me go first. I'm not complicated, fairly short story, not very interesting."

"Darla, I'm probably even more boring, I'll buy the next round and you can defer if you like, I'll keep my past brief. "

"Troy, how about real short past histories, and a quick lightning round of questions, then we can watch the game and make small talk, I'm a big fan of baseball."

"Ok Darla, sounds good, me, never been married, no kids, big baseball fan myself."

"Well Troy, never been married, no kids, in between jobs or careers as they say, sounds like a good start."

Troy and Darla drank and talked for about three hours. The bar was almost as empty when they got up to leave as it was when they met. Outside Slider lit up a cigarette, exhaled and took in the soft evening breeze. Darla stood close to him, looking at him eye to eye. She was as tall as he. She reached out and softly touched his face.

"I'll be staying on the boat for a few weeks, at least. Sort of house sitting, or as they say house boat sitting. Let's catch another game in a few nights, like to get to know you better."

"Yeah, sure, I good for it, I'm gonna work and stay here for a while, in this area. The room I rent is in a pretty seedy motel, so I'll pass on inviting you over, maybe we could catch lunch down on one of the dockside bars some afternoon."

"Hey, don't worry about your digs, I won't judge you on where you live. Don't be a stranger, goodnight Troy."

Darla walked away and glanced back and smiled at him one more time. Slider watched her perfect butt walk away, he wondered if she really wanted to see him again or was it the vodka martini's talking. He sure hoped for the former.

Chapter Forty-Nine

Spader and Olivia met for lunch at a little bar near Tioga in early August. Olivia updated him on her life so far in North Texas. She said that a local, she called him a cowboy, had showed some interest in her and she was considering going out with him. He came into the store occasionally to pick up feed, supplies for the ranch where he worked and he always made small talk with her. He was polite and seemed easy going. He had noticed a picture of Steele she had on her cell phone wallpaper and he had inquired about the dog. She reluctantly told him about the agility competitions and he said he was interested in watching her run him in the fall when she told him the trials would resume.

She also said that she had gone to the gun club in Frisco, taken some lessons and purchased a pistol. She chose a Sig Sauer 9mm. She was going to apply for her carry license as soon as she got her 6 months residency requirement in. Spader gave her Rick's snub nose 38 and she traded him his 12 gauge Remington for one in 20 gauge. She really didn't want to trade but she had realized that her grandfather and Spader were really close, plus it was apparent that Spader didn't have any agenda. He was honest and forthcoming and probably could have taken her for some of her grandfather's possessions if he wanted to. She wanted him to have her grandfather's old shotgun.

Spader said that he wanted to discuss the information about the PI agency that Rick had worked at.

"I probably over did this, you know, old man, limited contact and I was just glad someone gave me some time, listened to me. I never met you, but when I talk to you, I see my buddy Rick. His talk about you, the way he described you. I always thought he felt bad that he didn't keep enough contact with you, I guess guilt. I know I said that before, just repeating. Not sure about your aunt, he never talked much about her or his sister, not sure if she is even alive. He was closed mouthed about his family, marriage his parents. You are the only one that he seemed interested in, or maybe cared about. Not really sure."

Olivia paused and smiled, she liked this guy and realized that he was the only link to her family other than Kimberly.

"Don't worry, Vanderkelen said it was hard to determine a link when my grandfather was working for the PI, you know whether it had something to do with his murder."

Spader seemed to relax a little, it was obvious from his body language that this conversation stressed him a little.

"Rick never really talked about the PI stuff, he always played it off as nonsense stuff, checking on someone cheating on a wife, husband whatever. Hard to place blame today, seems people are never loyal to each other, or anyone for that matter. I said before, I think, there was at least one who was an AWOL from the military, I could never figure why the military went to a PI, but he never said anything about it. I always figured the PI might have been connected in some way, not sure how."

"Do you think he was picked because of his background, Army service stuff after he was discharged?"

"Your grandfather never said why he went on with him, them I mean. It is a as they say a mom and pop operation, well not quite."

"I never heard that, that term, mom and pop." Olivia laughed.

"Actually it is a retired cop and his daughter helps out with it. I guess it is a no brainer, but I would think that most PI's are ex cops, wasn't Vanderkelen an ex cop, he said he was retired."

Olivia thought about this and decided not to disclose the details on Vanderkelen's demise, decided to keep it simple. It was obvious that he kept it to himself when possible.

"Yeah, he was a homicide detective and a sheriff's deputy, in that order."

"Ok, not really that important, he has a website, says he has an office in Dallas and one in Denton. Probably one is out of his home, Rick said that the Denton office is on Dallas Street, just a store front in a small strip mall. You can get the addresses and numbers on the computer. Calls himself North Texas Investigations. Name is Schmidt."

"So what does this have to do with anything, was there something specific, something that my grandfather might have said that was unusual."

"Yeah, just one, right before he left for Florida, he said that he had to interview a young women for Schmidt. He said that she was of Vietnamese descent, her family, grandparents that is, came here after the war, but she was born here. I think her mother was Vietnamese but her father was an American. "

Olivia looked down, paused for a thought, then replied, "is that all, anything else?"

"He said that she spoke fluent Vietnamese, figured that her grandparents made her learn the language. Schmidt told him he could convince her to answer honestly because of his background and his ability to speak and understand Vietnamese."

"You know, it makes some sense, depends on what the information was that he wanted."

"Just remember Olivia, Schmidt is probably not allowed to talk about the case, I guess there is some confidential thing, you know law stuff, but it might be worth a try."

Olivia and Spader moved on to another topic but the whole time he thought that it might be worth a try to talk to Schmidt. The beer was cold and the barbecue tasty. Spader always ended their contacts by telling her how much of a good friend her grandfather was to him.

Chapter Fifty

Slider and Darla continued their relationship, meeting at bars, mostly Pete's, and an occasional lunch at the dock site. Slider was cautious at first but Darla charmed him into giving her some background, sketchy at best but enough information where she developed some theories about him. She was pretty sure that his name was an alias and his former occupation involved at least some illegal activity. She wasn't deterred and their relationship eventually progressed into a physical one. They often went to the houseboat, had sex, and Slider often stayed overnight.

Darla's past was much less complicated. Her family lived in the DC metro area. She had two sisters and a brother. All remained living and working near her parents. Darla's father was a lawyer for a Maryland law firm, her mom worked as a social worker in a school district. The siblings were all college educated with the exception of Darla.

Darla dropped out of several colleges and worked mostly service type jobs, all beneath the expectations of her family. She moved on, traveled and always made enough to support herself. She preferred warm climates and had worked for the family that owned the houseboat for the past four years. They trusted and liked her. They were very wealthy with several houses in Florida and South Carolina. Darla never questioned their wealth, but the family had disclosed that some of their money came from an inheritance. Darla had street smarts and had learned, partly from her employer, how to handle and invest her money. At 35 she had done very well for herself. Slider, or Troy as she knew him by, intrigued her. She was pretty sure she wanted to be in the relationship for the long haul. She was willing to accept whatever his past revealed.

Chapter Fifty-One

Olivia had trouble reaching Schmidt. He never returned her calls or e mails. After about two weeks she sent him a text message and he finally responded. He wanted to know the nature of her calls, she felt that he was trying to determine whether or not she was a "paying customer." Olivia figured that at least he wasn't hard up for clients.

Early one September morning Olivia drove to the Denton office address hoping she could catch him. The office was in a strip mall, eight storefronts, two of which were vacant. One tattoo parlor, a nail salon, real estate office, chicken take out joint, dry cleaning service and North Texas Investigations. She was in luck, the office was open and as she entered she was greeted by none other than Roy Schmidt himself. He was short, maybe 5'6" at best, probably 20 pounds overweight and completely bald. Schmidt was dressed in jeans that were a little too tight, a University North Texas polo shirt and dock siders with no socks. He was unarmed, but she noted an empty holster in plain sight on his desk. He was friendly and allowed her to give her opening as to why she was there. He made no excuses about not answering her phone calls or responding to her voice mail messages.

"The website lists my offices as in Dallas and here. Actually the Dallas office is in Plano. Just over the city line. You're lucky you caught me. I was just up here for a few hours tying up a few loose ends on some cases. I do remember your grandfather, he had a license and did some work for me. It's been a few years. I read about his death, nobody ever called me, I didn't figure it had anything to do with his work for me. He seemed like the type that guarded his personal matters. Like probably not many people even knew he worked for me. He helped me close a few deals, cases, you see, he did an interview here and there, I only met him face to face a few times. We mostly kept in touch through e mails, texts. He was pretty easy going, I liked him, and what he did for me was good stuff."

Olivia raised her hand to stop him, "anything serious that you think he could have been killed for."

"It was all pretty easy stuff, my oldest daughter got her license and she handles that stuff for me now, part time, she also works over at UNT," he smiled and pointed at the logo on his golf shirt.

Olivia asked again, "anything risky, or maybe dangerous, I'm just trying to figure out why he was killed, it's a cold case with the police."

"I wouldn't give my daughter anything risky, and I felt the same way about Rick, your grandfather. I don't even give myself risky stuff." Schmidt laughed and shook his head. "you know this business ain't like on TV."

Olivia raised an eyebrow, "look, I wasn't insinuating anything, just wondering. A friend of his said he interviewed a young Vietnamese women for you right before he was murdered, I was wondering about the nature of that interview."

Roy Schmidt shook his head again, "look, you know can't just open a file and discuss it with you, my reputation is at stake if I did. But I'm really in the dark about this."

Olivia raised her voice and moved closer to Roy, she realized that she was about a head taller than him, "what do you mean."

"It wasn't my case, it was a favor, we pawn stuff off occasionally to other PI's. But it has to work both ways, like they say vice a versa. This came from one in Paris, not France, Paris Texas. She, Melanie, called me and asked for a favor. Her and I occasionally exchange favors on cases. She knew that I had used Rick and I had told her that he spoke Vietnamese. One of the reasons I liked him, there is a small Vietnamese population in North Texas, not as big as the Houston area, but enough to have that ability as an edge."

"Then what was it about, why did she need him to interview this women."

"I don't know, I didn't even open a file on it, I gave her his info and left it at that. She got back to me about a month later, just to touch base, said he did it for her and she passed the interview on. I left it at that."

"Is she still around, did you see the interview, or talk to him about it."

"Oh yeah," Schmidt walked around to his desk and pulled a business card out of the top drawer, he handed it to Olivia, you can keep it, she gave me a few, we exchanged cards, good to have resources in this business. On the second part, no I never discussed the interview with him or Melanie. She did say he did a good job and was satisfied. She settled up, you know paid him herself, I never got involved in any of that."

Olivia examined the card, and then looked up at Schmidt. "Ok is this still good contact information."

"Yeah, I just used her about a month ago, she's good, a retired homicide detective, Philadelphia PD. Call her, maybe she will discuss this with you. Where do you live?"

"Pilot Point."

"Paris isn't that far, North East of the Dallas, not as far as Paris France," Schmidt chuckled and wished her good luck.

When Olivia left she realized that she never asked Schmidt if he was ever contacted by Woodruff or Vanderkelen. She figured she could double back on that at a later date.

$$\textsf{Chapter Fifty-Two}$$

livia didn't want to wait too long. She had an idea that all of this was going nowhere, but she wanted to follow through with it. In the meantime her cowboy, Gar Riley, had pressed a little more and she relented and went out with him. Gar was 29, about 5' 10" tall and on the lean side. He wasn't a homegrown Texan, actually born and raised in the southwestern Virginia area. After High School he joined the Army, did a tour in Afghanistan, got out and was stationed at Fort Hood until his discharge. He liked Texas and after his discharge went to the University of North Texas where he graduated with a degree in Agricultural Sciences. He took a job at a local ranch as a ranch hand. He wanted to start from the ground up so he accepted the entry level job. He never regretted his decision and decided to make Texas, specifically North Texas, his home.

He was smitten with Olivia from the first time he had seen her in the store. A little on the shy side, and not real flashy it took him a while to ask her out. She was relieved when he finally did and wondered why it took him so long. They took in a UNT football game in Denton and afterwards had a drink at a local bar. They made small talk, Olivia wanted him to do most of the talking as she wanted to avoid getting too far into her background early on. Apparently Gar was in the same frame of mind and the conversation was somewhat awkward. On some levels they hit it off, but both were cautious, and for this Olivia was thankful. Although she was interested, moving slow was fine with her. They ended the evening parting ways at the parking lot of the club, as they had agreed to meet at the game with their own vehicles. Olivia's FJ and Gar's slightly worn Chevy Silverado pickup. Just before parting Gar told her he would like to see her again, Olivia agreed and they both parted smiling. Olivia thought that for one moment it looked like he was going to try and kiss her. She wished he had.

Chapter Fifty-Three

It didn't take long for Olivia to get a hold of Melanie Stefanik. Prior to calling Olivia researched her on line. Her website gave a brief bio and there were a few articles that she was able to pull up on the internet. She learned that Melanie had been involved in a shooting while serving as a detective for Philadelphia PD. She and her partner had walked into a drug deal gone bad while attempting to locate a witness on another case. Knocking on doors in North Philadelphia can be dangerous. Melanie and her partner identified themselves to the men and they began firing at the two detectives. Melanie returned fire and wounded one of the suspects while sustaining a wound to her shoulder. Her partner probably saved her life, as he was able to pull her out of the way while returning fire to the suspects. He killed one in the exchange of gun fire.

There was some push back though from the liberal media and politicians from the Mayor's office. The dead suspect was shot in the back, in what appeared to be an effort to get away. He did not have a gun in his possession when the responding investigators looked at the crime scene. The incident took place in one of the drug infested North Philadelphia neighborhoods just before dusk. The anti- law enforcement advocates claimed that the suspect should not have been shot, since they felt he was unarmed. The two remaining suspects, including the wounded one, were later captured. Both were anxious to cut deals with the DA and gave statements to the effect that the dead man's 40 caliber hand gun was removed by the suspects in the confusion and later discarded. Neither suspect was willing to own up to taking the gun, each pointed the finger at the other. The gun was never recovered and the media and protesters were never satisfied and claimed a cover up based on racial issues.

Melanie took her pension under the union contract guidelines regarding an officer wounded in the line of duty. The articles were very slanted, a reflection of the Philadelphia newspaper and media bias towards the Philadelphia PD. The union defended both detectives, but the divide in the city continued to fester and only got worse.

Olivia called Melanie and was surprised at her reception. They made arrangements to meet at Melanie's home outside of Paris, Texas. Melanie told her she was willing to talk to her about her grandfather, but it was a long story. Olivia was instructed to go through Paris on Route 82 and proceed towards Clarksville. Melanie lived about two miles past Paris just off of Route 82.

Chapter Fifty-Four

Olivia planned for a long day. The trip was easy, just the reverse of her trip to Texas only East on 82 instead of West. She arrived at about 11 AM and drove down the long gravel driveway that led to a large brick and stone ranch house. The property was fenced and contained a small stable, a large detached garage and what looked like privacy fenced in pool area just behind house.

Melanie greeted her at the door and asked her in. Olivia had dressed casually, her normal nonworking attire, denim shorts, running shoes and an oversized black pocket t shirt. Melanie was short, petite and appeared to be in her mid- fifties, but Olivia was bad on guessing age. She had short brown hair, blue eyes and was dressed in tan cargo shorts and a black denim snap button western shirt. She had the sleeves rolled up to her elbows.

"Come on in, we can sit in the den or out by the pool, not real hot today, where ever you are comfortable."

Olivia responded, "I'll leave it up to you, wherever you feel like."

After a few preliminary exchanges Melanie started what was going to be a long conversation.

"Ok, first just a short history, I'll assume you looked me up and know my history with Philadelphia PD. My first husband and I were divorced before I took my pension. He was a cop too and had a roving eye. I had already met Dean, we married and moved out here. He is an engineer and what you might say semi- retired but does some consulting. We bought this property as is, it was formerly a working ranch. We have been re doing it a bit at a time. Dean was the one who talked me into getting the PI license, good move. I work less but make more money than when I was a Philly cop. Just wanted to get that out of the way."

"While we are getting stuff out of the way, whatever happened to your partner, when you were a detective?"

"He survived, he was pretty close to pension when I got shot. He stuck it out and took his pension on the first opportunity. He took a lot of shit for what happened. Funny, you get jammed up like that and they make you a villain for just trying to defend yourself, doing your job. We just were at the wrong place at the wrong time. The witness we were looking for had nothing to do with the drug deal or the suspects in the shooting. The bad guys, in this case, drug dealers with extensive jackets, long histories of crime, all got time in prison. They were made out to be the victims, we were, according to the media the bad guys. It's like they think that when you are under fire, being shot at, you shouldn't have the option to shoot back, you should just de- escalate. Like to see what the politicians and media types would do under fire. Anyway, my partner, he saved my life, pulled me out of the line of fire, completely exposed himself. They found over 40 shell casings on the scene, and between me and him we only fired 9 shots."

They moved to the den and Olivia sat in an old leather chair that you sort of sink into, rather than sat on. The furniture and decorations were all in western motif, the ceiling had exposed beams that looked like they might have been a hundred years old. There was a small bar in the corner, with stools that looked like they came out of an old western saloon. Behind the bar was a small flat screen TV, the only modern touch to the whole room.

"Dean is originally from Texas, he graduated from A and M. He has sort of made me a Texan, best moves of my whole life, Dean and Texas."

"Doesn't he worry about you, you know PI all of that."

"I don't take anything risky at all. Most of my stuff is pretty routine, nothing in the city, Dallas I mean. I still carry, everywhere I go. Dean carries also. It's a Texas thing. The shoulder still hurts, a little pain, I adjusted and gave up the cop gun. Use a Smith and Wesson 380 now."

Olivia adjusted her position and declined an offer for coffee.

Melanie continued. "Roy gave me a heads up about you. He's a real charmer, you know, I send him anything I'm not comfortable with."

Olivia paused and then sort of interrupted, "sorry but he was awful hard to get a hold of, what's with that."

"Oh, hey he is a real good investigator. He was also a good cop, had a stellar reputation. You know don't let the appearance fool you. A lot of them, the PI's, think they are TV or movie stars. Roy is not flashy, but he is good, and he has way more work than he can handle. Gets a lot of stuff other guys, and girls screw up. I think your grandfather liked him, at least respected him, respect is hard to get these days."

"Did you ever meet my grandfather?"

"No, just talked on the phone and exchanged e mails. Roy hooked us up, he was perfect for this case, I guess now we can get down to business."

Olivia smiled, Melanie was very at ease and obviously at no hurry.

"Let me say that I can't discuss what was in the interview, the content that is. You see I want to talk about it, I took an interest in this, let me start there. Because I am an ex or former

Philly detective, which ever you prefer, I occasionally get a referral from the area. Most of them I turn down, Dean doesn't want me to get into high profile stuff, I don't either. "

Melanie continued, "years ago there was a high profile case in Philly, it involved an abortion doctor who was performing full term abortions in his clinic. Now I am a prochoice advocate, you know first trimester, its ok, the women's choice, control over her body, I believe in all that. But this guy was snipping full term births. I mean he was using scissors and snipping the spine at the back of their necks. Long story but you can google it. I knew one of the detectives who worked the case. Anyway, the doctor was convicted of first degree murder on 5 counts, and he refused any appeal rights if they took the death penalty off of the table. That's got to tell you something, like let's face it he knew he was guilty. This caused a lot of friction between the prolife and the prochoice factions in the city. The prochoice people had an ally. A state congressional representative from a county that borders the city supported and encouraged prochoice harassment of the prolife people. On more than one occasion he participated in the harassment. He claims to be an advocate of the downtrodden, but he is nothing more than a thug from a privileged background. He is a lawyer, but always remember, good lawyers don't work for the government or become politicians. He was sleeping with a young women of Vietnamese descent. Her mother is Vietnamese and her father an American. I think Roy said he told you that much. Well, in addition to any knowledge she might have had regarding her boyfriend's involvement in the prolife harassment there were also some domestic violence complaints against him. He leaned on the police and of course that went away. Local suburban cops, they can be bought off as easy as any corrupt city cops. Depends on their political leanings, and like the city this particular suburb is very liberal. Liberal politician, liberal local government, they press the cops, it goes away. Anyway, eventually a law suit is filed, this high profile firm files against the prochoice people and city on the basis of harassment and the city not protecting the prolife people, when they have protests or any dialogue with the citizens. And the girl, she disappears. An investigator for the law firm traces her, gets her cell phone records and determines she is in North Texas. That is where me and your grandfather come in."

Olivia was riveted to the story, she held her hand up to get a question in. "What about the girls family, weren't they trying to locate her, weren't they upset."

"That is another conflict, her family, that is, her grandparents are from Vietnam. The grandparents came over after the fall of Saigon. They got relocated in the Philadelphia area, raised a family and eventually became very successful. The girl's aunt and an uncle own three high end and successful Vietnamese restaurants in Philly. The aunt is married to the owner or general manager, not sure which one, of one of the professional sports franchises in Philly. Can't remember which team but it doesn't matter. I'm not a sports fan, Dean and I occasionally take in an A and M football game, but that's about it. Dean, being an engineer leans more towards motorsports and away from stick and ball stuff. Ok with me, I've become a racing fan also. I've digressed here, let me get back on topic. Anyway the guy, the owner or manager of the team, he's a high profile guy in the area. So there is probably pressure on him from the liberal politicians. You know, money stuff, contracts for stadiums, city revenue appropriations, stuff like that."

"So you think they would jeopardize one of their own, to please some rich guy and his wife who owns a sports team."

"Olivia, don't get ahead of me here, they probably got her out of there, for her own safety, and to avoid her testifying. And also maybe kill two birds with one stone, she disappears is safe, she is away from the abusive creep of a boyfriend and they don't have to get involved. They didn't count on someone like your grandfather finding her."

"How did he find her, where was she, where is she now, I had read where she had been missing."

"Ok, lots to cover here, let's take a break, I'll make lunch and we can sit out by the pool and finish this. I told you, it is a long story, and some of it is me speculating, or as they say trying to follow the evidence."

Chapter Fifty-Five

Melanie made sandwiches while Olivia sat outside by the pool. The pool was completely fenced in, 8ft. high privacy fence. The poolside furniture was wrought iron with black and white stripped cushions. It was sunny now, but a slow moving breeze made it quite comfortable. Melanie brought the sandwiches out and offered her a beer.

"I drink wine mostly, Dean drinks beer, prefers domestic but stays away from light beers. He says if you are going to drink beer, drink real beer not watered down beer. He also has some Mexican imports, so pick your poison."

"I'll have whatever he drinks on the domestic side, whatever is easy."

Melanie came back with two bottles of Coors Banquet and they settled in for the rest of Melanie's story.

"When your grandfather and I touched base all we had was her cell phone number, which by this time had been discarded. I'm sure the family knew where she was but played dumb. The girl, Lian, probably went to burners for communication."

Melanie continued, " he was good, I knew he could speak Vietnamese and that he had served in Vietnam, so I wasn't surprised, that is surprised that he was so successful. Within two and a half weeks he had a finished interview submitted to me via e mail. He actually got more than the lawyers even asked for, which again didn't surprise me, but I am sure it surprised them."

"Where, or should I say how did he find her." Olivia wiped her face with a napkin, the sandwiches were delicious but a bit sloppy. She took a gulp of the beer and looked back in the direction of Melanie.

"He found her in a Vietnamese restaurant in Frisco. The only thing he wasn't able to do was get an address, she wasn't going to tell him who she was living with or where."

"Didn't the owners try and protect her, I mean from being interviewed."

"He really never said about any resistance, Roy had described him as being in good shape and kind of intimidating. So I'm sure he would have been able to take care of whoever was watching over her. She's was only 21, so probably doesn't have any issues with the family controlling her."

"How long did it take, where did it take place."

"He told me over the phone that they talked outside the restaurant, it has a patio, and it wasn't busy, he caught her late morning but before the lunch crowd started. About an hour, you know first breaking the ice, trying to gain her trust, I sure he was a skilled interviewer. I figure if the Army sent him to language school they put his skills to work, like that is what I figure he did. Interview or interrogate the enemy. He said she spoke English well, but played dumb at first, until she realized he was able to understand and communicate in Vietnamese.

Olivia sat back and tried to collect her thoughts, "I read where she was missing, do you think she is dead."

"No, the family probably moved her to another location, somewhere in another Vietnamese community. I know that the immigrants from the war have bonded in various places and tried to retain their own culture. This probably satisfies the family and the prochoice bunch, she is hidden, alive but doesn't ever appear to testify."

"How important would it be for the prolife people to have her testify."

"I don't know Olivia, I read the interview and it appears as though they were looking at the guy she was living with. A good lawyer probably would have any testimony regarding the relationship kept out of court, but maybe they thought about leaks."

"I don't get it, how does that help the case of the prolife people."

"Look, the guy is a prochoice, liberal asshole or as they call themselves progressives. But on the other hand he had DV issues with Lian, so it probably pisses off the "me too" movement. There is an Attorney General in the Midwest, I can't remember the state, but he was the same thing, a liberal who was beating his girlfriend. They, the progressives covered it up but almost cost him the election."

"How would that help, I don't see it."

"It taints his credibility, you know a politician and pro-choice advocate who beats his girlfriend, they would have figured a way to get it in. There was also a few other points in the interview I think would have helped them, but I have already told you too much."

"So do you think that this got my grandfather killed."

"I don't know, but I talked to both Woodruff and Vanderkelen. Maybe they, whoever killed him, feared that he would disclose the contents of the interview. I have seen people killed for less, witnesses, people who were hired by the police, you know informants. "

"Neither Vanderkelen or Woodruff mentioned talking to you to me, why."

"I don't know, they are cops, they learn to say as little as possible to satisfy collaterals in their cases. I have to give Woodruff the benefit of the doubt. It wasn't his case, they admitted that the detective who caught it wasn't very good. The crime scene was compromised, not the deputy's fault, just that he was unprepared, the call seemed to be a BS thing. The only person in that department who would have known what to do was Vanderkelen, and he was a shamed ex detective who had been thrown out of his own department and sent there as a deputy on the night shift to finish out his pension."

Olivia paused then smiled, "I read about him, Woodruff clued me but didn't say much."

"Yeah, he let his dick get him into trouble, I call it cop fever. You know it's all about pussy. My ex was the same way, always following his dick."

Melanie continued.

"I read where there was an attempt to kill the lawyer who was handling the law suit against the city, but the press said it was an attempted robbery."

"You don't think it was the same guy, you know the one who killed my grandfather."

"That's a stretch, but if it was they wouldn't be that stupid, and if they were, which I doubt, I am sure that he has been eliminated. You know most of those hired hit men have a short shelf life."

"It's been worth the trip, Melanie, I need to start thinking about going home. Got two dogs that are missing me."

"You know Olivia, it's the cop in me, but I did a little research on you, and I know about the dog stuff, agility. A girlfriend of mine back east does that, she's actually pretty good, has border collies. I called her, she said she saw you run in Orlando, said you were pretty good. I won't name her, but she also admired your good looks, she is that way, you know, gay."

Olivia blushed at the compliment, felt a little awkward about being attractive to another female, but she had previously experienced this at agility trials.

"I'm still pretty new, but like it and intend on continuing."

Chapter Fifty-Six

Melanie picked up the empty bottles and offered to show Olivia out. It had gotten warmer and Melanie showed her the old barn on their way to Olivia's FJ.

"Dean and I are going to update the barn, it has good bones but has been neglected. Being an engineer he has all kinds of plans, most of which he can accomplish himself. He has taught me some carpentry and I like it. When we finish I am going to board some horses and we will probably own a few. Being from Texas Dean likes to ride. I'll learn, I'm not afraid of them. We plan to put an RV shelter up in the back of the barns, he wants to restore a used RV. He is always looking for new projects. It's the engineer in him. I really lucked out with him, such a change from my ex, can't believe it."

"If you ever want a dog, give me a call, I am always running across people who are looking for rescue prospects."

"Thanks Olivia, I was going to mention that was on my, our, to do list but forgot. If you have any more questions, call me, keep in touch, you are really not that far away."

Olivia smiled, she liked Melanie, "thanks, I will, I appreciate your sharing all this with me."

"One more thing, don't try and solve this, there are so many unsolved homicides and it seems to be moving in that direction, like so many go unsolved. This was a hit. I said before the guy who did it is probably dead, and if not eventually he will be killed, probably by his own people if he screws one up. Live your life, you are young and have your whole future ahead of you. And trust me, I can tell even from my brief contact with Rick, your grandfather, that he was a remarkable man. Just savor that, don't beat yourself up over his murder."

With that Olivia bid Melanie goodbye and headed back on 82 West towards home.

Chapter Fifty-Seven

By middle of September Darla had located a new job, another house boat sitting situation for friends of her current employer. There were no hard feelings and she had made up her mind. She wanted to move on. Naturally she wanted Slider to move on with her. He had revealed more of his background and Darla filled in the blanks. She was not deterred and convinced him that they could make a life together.

Port Charlotte Harbor was further south and a more affluent area. This presented a problem for Slider, as the local marinas wanted ID's, SSAN information and even references for their help. Pay was by check and taxes submitted to the Fed. Slider knew he was never going to collect Social Security or obtain Medicare, but he figured with his background he wasn't going to lose sleep over it. While working at the marina near Largo, he had detailed a few boats for locals. He learned that the wealthy usually weren't interested in doing physical labor. So he and Darla hatched a plan where he could detail boats on a cash basis and start by word of mouth. Both were surprised when it ended up being steady employment. He even got to the point of having business cards made up, "DETAILING BY TROY", along with a cell phone number billed to Darla.

Prior to leaving the Largo area they had the Jeep titled in Darla's name complete with legitimate owners card and Florida license plates. Darla's friends had connections and everything was above board. The Jeep was repainted, had some minor body work done and was good to go. One less worry when driving around. Slider even had a Florida driver's license issued under one of his "clean" names.

Darla took a job at a local pub, earned the trust of the owner's and within months was managing the bar. Troy's business turned out to be more lucrative than they both expected. Darla handled the money and after discussion with Troy invested some of the profits. Their relationship blossomed and Darla never once tried to pry too far into his past. Except for work relationships they pretty much kept to themselves, both preferring it that way.

Chapter Fifty-Eight

The Ashville North Carolina area was fast becoming a land developers dream. Parts of Western North Carolina was a hot spot for over 55 housing developments. It was advertised as the fastest growing retirement area in the country. Some of the large tracts of land had been obtained from landowners, farmers and local privately owned campgrounds. The holdouts were constantly solicited by buyers for the land developers and building contractors.

Just north of Hendersonville on the way to Ashville was one such campground. The location consisted of rental cabins, house trailers and old RV's converted to stationary shelters. The rent was cheap and few questions were asked. In the middle of October a decomposing body was discovered in a trailer that was thought to have been vacant at the time. The body was tagged in the county coroner's facility as a John Doe.

No identification was found and the samples taken for possible identification were awaiting the lab results. Local authorities classified the death as suspicious, but the crime scene yielded no evidence. The John Doe had died from a gunshot wound to the head, but no shell casings were found. The county coroner concluded that the round was probably a 9MM and the shot was at close range. He also concluded that the victim died approximately 10 days prior to being discovered. The campground owners told investigators that the trailer was unoccupied and was scheduled to be sold for scrap. Investigators were unable to find any recent missing persons reports fitting the description of victim.

As it turned out, unbeknownst to the local authorities, John Doe's crime, if you want to call it that, was his close resemblance to a professional hit man known by the code name of Slider. Investigator's combed the area for witnesses. None of the occupants of the nearby cabins or RV's could supply any information. Nobody heard gunshots, nobody was aware that anyone was living in the trailer and nobody witnessed any comings or going from the trailer. One witness said that she observed an argument outside a restaurant on route 26 a couple of weeks or so before the body had been discovered. She had difficulty time framing her observation but said that two large men dressed in suits were arguing about the identity of "someone they popped." She said that she dismissed it because they were scary looking and appeared to be what she referred to as "being impaired." She could not identify a vehicle and only that both had dark hair, sunglasses, dark suits and were "somewhat overweight."

Another investigation probably headed for the cold case file.

Chapter Fifty-Nine

Olivia returned to her work and training routine. She also started running on the track at one of the local High Schools. She was always fast and had endurance but figured it would only enhance her ability to run her dogs. The training facility added a second trainer for the agility program. Because she was fairly new as a client she was reassigned to the new trainer.

This was a good thing, another perspective and this trainer was a man. He had extensive experience and like Olivia ran a breed that was not considered a natural for agility. They hit it off and she liked his calm manner and the fact that he was humble. He spent the training sessions working on skills, not bragging about his accomplishments or his dogs. The other teams in her class seemed to like him also. He had a unique ability to instruct at the level of the student / dog team. This helped the progress of both Steele and JD.

Steele was definitely ready to start qualifying consistently at the master's level. He was probably able to gain some placements on a good run. JD wasn't ready for competition yet but made progress and seemed to have potential. This is where Kyle, her new trainer seemed to excel. He was able to take the little steps with the dog and handler and determine when the team was confident enough to move to the next task. In all it was working well.

There were local trials coming up and she wanted to enter both dogs and hoped that JD would be ready for novice. Kyle suggested that she enter JD in a class called Fast. It allowed the handler to structure the run to the dog's skills and it was often used by handlers to train for the Jumpers with Weaves and Standard classes. Entering her would also give JD the opportunity to get used to the atmosphere of trialing. The noises, the fact that the dogs were crated or confined between runs and the opportunity to further socialize a "green" dog. A definite plus for anyone considering competing with a dog.

Even with the return to work and the training the mystery surrounding the death of her grandfather was rarely absent from her mind. She thought about the discussions with Spader, Linda Rossi and Melanie Stefanik. She often wondered about John Price. The information from Eddie regarding her grandfather's job in Vietnam allowed her to see some similarities in the book that Price had written. She took the time to read the book again. In her opinion it was somewhat of a stretch, but the subject matter of the book resembled her grandfather's job as described by Spader. But after all it was fiction.

Olivia was thankful for the opportunity to have a relationship with Spader. This was probably the only real link to her grandfather. They routinely saw each other, had a few beers and maybe lunch or dinner. Spader taught her Texas and Oklahoma or has he called it Texoma culture and lore. To make things easier on both they decided to introduce Spader as her uncle. This way they could avoid any conversation about the relationship between Spader and Rick. This also helped Spader who was always uncomfortable discussing Vietnam. Olivia was taken back when he told her that she could call him Spade, a name previously reserved for her grandfather.

Chapter Sixty

Thanksgiving morning, 2018. The early morning Texas sun had just started to peek through the blinds. Olivia quietly slipped out of bed and pulled on a pair of grey sweatpants on the floor next to the bed. She couldn't find her panties in the darkness, they were entwined in the pile of clothes at the side of the bed. She straightened her golf shirt with the logo Agility Invitational, Orlando FL 2017. The twin bed was crowded with two, when she moved in she had only thought about sleeping alone. She liked the closeness of his body. She looked at him, Gar was sleeping softly, he was usually up and gone by 6AM to the ranch where he worked. It was nice to have him to share breakfast with. She quietly left the bedroom and let both Steele and JD out for a potty break and then brought them in and fed them. Next she put on coffee and started cooking eggs and bacon.

This would be her first attempt at a dinner, Thanksgiving yet, for someone other than herself. Gar had brought two pies baked by the wife of one of the owners of the ranch where he worked. They wanted to help him impress his "little Florida girlfriend." She invited Spader for dinner, but he refused. She was able to talk him into coming later in the day for dessert. He agreed and it made her happy. Steele and JD both with full stomachs had gone back to their respective dog beds, Steele in one of the spare bedrooms, JD in the corner of the living room.

She was smiling and admiring the progress on the house. Gar had installed a new kitchen floor, ceramic tile. As it turned out he was quite handy, one of his many positive attributes. She heard the toilet flush in the bathroom off of the master bedroom, he was awake. Their lovemaking last night was slow and meaningful. She got butter flies in her stomach thinking about it. Today would be slow and easy. Tomorrow Gar would go back to work and she had an agility trial in Frisco. Both dogs were entered tomorrow, just Steele on Saturday and Sunday.

Gar entered the kitchen, put his arms up and yawned. He had a University of North Texas T shirt, faded Levi jeans and was barefoot. His slightly sun bleached brown hair was pulled back into a short pony tail. Olivia was as tall as him, with both being barefoot. Gar kissed her slowly and smiled.

"Are you ready to be my cooking guinea pig, first time big meal for a man."

Gar smiled, "ok, yeah, but first what is for breakfast," he laughed.

Olivia laughed, pulled him towards her and kissed him, not so softly. "that's gratitude, I'm talking about dinner, Thanksgiving yet and you want breakfast too, well sit down bacon and eggs will have to do. After breakfast stay out of my way, this is a big project for me."

Gar poured himself a cup of coffee, and sat down at the kitchen island.

"Hey is your Uncle Eddie, I sure he is really not your uncle, coming for dinner."

"No, but he agreed to come down for dessert later in the day, I think he might make it."

"Do you think he is lonely, you know, who wants to spend Thanksgiving alone."

"Someday I will explain how we are sort of related, and yes he is a loner, but not lonely. Had his share of relationships along the way, but nothing that stuck."

Olivia placed the bacon and eggs in front of Gar and continued. "sometimes people get tired of relationships and just move on by themselves."

Gar carefully carved up the pieces of bacon, "so maybe you are basing this on your experiences, you know, you don't say much about your past."

Olivia smiled, deep down she liked his concern but felt it was too early to play her hand, it wasn't a game to her, she wanted to proceed carefully. "Gar, you are laid back, easy going and I like the pace, but come on, don't complain, I am sleeping with you right."

Gar smiled, he caught on and decided to move on, he heard what he wanted, he definitely wanted this relationship to move on. "You left your panties on the side of the bed, so I guess there is nothing on under those sweats."

"You guessed right, I would show you but I want to finish making my breakfast and get moving on with Thanksgiving dinner."

"Ok, what can I help you with."

"Gar, nothing, this is my project, you can watch some parades on TV if you like."

"Not something I am interested in."

"One thing, after the stores open take a ride to the liquor store on 380 and get some wine."

"Neither one of us drinks wine, so why."

"This is a special occasion, ask one of the clerks for a suggestion for two people who are not sure what goes with turkey. Get something good, make sure it has a cork, no twist off caps, also get beer, imported, you pick it."

"Not Lone Star."

"Yeah, you know don't knock Lone Star, something different for Thanksgiving, I will need to unwind."

"What does Eddie drink."

"Budweiser, but I always keep some here, he occasionally drops by."

"How early are you going tomorrow."

"Tomorrow I will be up and gone before you, have to set up and all that."

"How did you get three days off in a row, this is a busy time."

"I volunteered for both Christmas Eve and New Year's Eve, I know both days will probably be early closings, but everyone wants that time off."

"You trade with some others in the store, sounds like you got the short end."

"Not really, this is the only chance for a while to run on turf, all the other local trials are on dirt. Steele has been on turf before, JD, well we will see. The place is supposed to be pretty good, indoor soccer facility."

Olivia sat down and started on her eggs, took a sip of coffee and looked at Gar who was sitting next to her at the kitchen island.

"On Sunday how bout I come over and watch you a while, I won't get in the way, I promise. Anyway I want to see you in your agility outfit, you know the spandex running stuff, all that."

"Come on Gar, you've seen me naked, nothing left to the imagination."

"Just kidding, I'll come over after I make my rounds at the ranch."

"Oh Gar, by the way, when you go to the liquor store take one of the dogs with you, they are both good travelers, you can take the FJ if you want."

"Which one."

Take JD, she'll like it. Steele he would go, but he could care less, sort of a loner himself."

Chapter Sixty-One

January 2019. Port Charlotte Harbor had worked well for Slider and Darla. The boat detailing business took off. He was good at what he did and often helped the owners, mostly wealthy people with too many activities and responsibilities, with advice and care for their boats. He and Darla managed to locate and buy a vintage Chris Craft cabin cruiser that had been partially restored. The boat was in dry dock and in his spare time Slider worked on making it functional.

It was a labor of love for him. The long term plan was for them to start a day fishing charter for a small number of patrons. They figured they could safely take out 4 or 5 a day, and maybe make 2 to 3 runs a week. They could live on the boat in a pinch as the houseboat sitting would eventually dry up. They figured with the charter, the detailing business and maybe Darla working part time at a bar they would have a pretty comfortable life style. Hard work, yes, but neither shied away from the challenge.

Slider and Darla went out on a few charters with various Captains at the marina, paid close attention to details and figured they could do this, just on a smaller scale. Slider was impressed that Darla easily became proficient at not only fishing but the various activities she would have to perform as his mate. They figured they might have to employ one other person on a part time basis.

They had met only six months prior and sooner or later Slider figured he would have to disclose at least part of his job history. He wanted to make sure that she was aware before they got too deeply involved in not only the relationship but also any business venture. He let her handle and keep almost all of the money, only taking a small amount from his detailing business to cover basic expenses. She never questioned this as she figured he just wasn't confident enough in his own ability to handle the finances. He had actually done very well on that front when he was "on the job."

When it came down to the discussion about his former vocation he was pleasantly surprised. She said that she figured he was previously involved in criminal behavior and wasn't surprised as to the extent. Her ability to read people was almost uncanny and she had even surmised that he had money stashed, and that he probably had more than one identity. She wasn't afraid of him and never doubted his honesty when it came to their relationship.

Darla told Slider that her father and the law firm he worked for sometimes defended people involved in organized crime and most likely were aware of situations where murders for hire had been committed. She said that her father often bragged about how corruption and crime paid and she always felt that her own father was probably very corrupt. Her siblings stayed in the area and two were in local politics and as she put it, "always on the take."

Her brother followed in the father's footsteps and became a lawyer. He worked for a DC law firm that was affiliated with lobbyist who represented various labor unions. Darla told Slider that he was even more corrupt than her father and took pleasure in promoting causes that ripped off the average person. All things said she decided that striking out on her own and working at honest jobs made her feel better about herself. She had little or no contact with her family. Her work ethic and ability to handle, save and invest money made for a modest but yet comfortable lifestyle. At the end of the day she assured Slider, who she called Troy that his past was just that, past. They worked and blended in with the with the Port Charlotte Harbor community.

Chapter Sixty-two

Tuesday, January 29, 2019. Olivia loaded Steele and JD into the FJ. It was early, she had an 8 AM class with Steele and a 9AM class with JD. The training center was only about 20 minutes away from her home. She had her I phone connected to the audio system of the FJ. She listened to a medley of songs by Waylon Jennings, Jessie Coulter, Margo Price and Hank Williams Jr. Her adaptation to North Texas covered all phases of her life. Kyle was a stickler for being on time but she was ahead of schedule. Long range weather forecast for far North Texas was for another cold winter with temperatures below average for January and February. It was brisk, cloudy, and wet. It had rained most of the night but it looked like the sun was trying to peek through.

She was due in at work by noon and would have to stay until 7PM. Long day if you included the two training sessions. There were three trials coming up in the next four weeks. All on dirt and she was looking forward to the challenge. Steele had done well in late November on turf. He qualified in 4 of 6 possible runs and earned almost 60 MACH points. JD had surprised her in the FAST class and ran pretty well considering it was her first attempt. Most important the chaos of the trial atmosphere didn't bother her. As one of the other handlers commented, "is she this chill at home." Olivia was relieved, this was half the battle, the skills would come in time.

Gar had talked her into the annual super bowl party at the ranch where he worked. A lot of the staff from her job would be there along with the ranch owners and their families. She had bought a new outfit for the party, a skirt, which was kind of short, and a matching blouse. She wanted to surprise him and look nice. She knew he wanted to show her off but he never let on. He was growing on her fast, it scared her a little, he was now staying overnight 3 or 4 times a week. But he was moving slow and always seemed to know when she needed a little space. He was great with the dogs and very supportive of her sport. Most important was the fact he always made her smile. Even though Tuesdays were hectic with training and work she asked Gar to come over after she was finished with her shift. He agreed and volunteered to bring some takeout so she didn't have to cook. She was starting to develop a taste for Mexican food, and there were a number of good restaurants in the area. It was early in the day and she was already looking forward to seeing him.

Spader was still a source of support for her. He occasionally dropped in or called and asked her to meet him. Gar and Spader seemed to hit it off. Both veterans, different wars but still cut from the same cloth. On one occasion Spader told her that Rick would have liked Gar "an awful lot." It almost made her feel as though it came from her grandfather. Spader was unique and Olivia was sure there was so much good in his head but most of it would probably never get out.

Olivia was never able to put the mystery of her grandfather's death out of her mind. Despite this frustration she realized that it had an upside. She was able to pick up and move, and to a place that she instantly loved. She often felt as though the transition was so smooth because she had no expectations. She accepted North Texas as it was, and it fit her perfectly. She continued with the dog sport, she knew and accepted Spader for what he was. That important link to her grandfather, which in turn was a link to her life. Then there was Gar. She wasn't afraid of her relationship with him going down the road.

She was also contemplating getting a PI license. She had researched the process on line and she could meet the qualifications. She spoke with Melanie who agreed to help her if she wanted to pursue it. Melanie also said that Roy Schmidt was willing to help her out. She even discussed it with Gar, who agreed and said he would support her. She believed him. Gar was easy to read. She didn't want it to solve her grandfather's murder, but her interest in the case had peaked something inside her.

All of this ran through her mind as she pulled into the training center on Red Tail Hawk road. Both dogs had perked up, as they always did when she got close to the center. Now it was time to have some fun. Steele wasn't a border collie, she wasn't ever going to the world team, but she accepted him for what he was. A hard working dog who always gave her everything he had. JD, well, who knows, most important she was having fun with her dogs.

ONE YEAR LATER

Slider and Darla made the move in the fall of 2019. Port Charlotte Harbor gave way to Plantation Key. Plantation Key is one of six islands that makes up Islamorada Key. The travel and destination brochures and on line advertising describe it as follows: "Perhaps the world's highest density of professional off charter boats with tournament grade captains can be found in Islamorada of 6 islands where the backcountry sport fishing and salt water fly fishing were pioneered."

Neither were deterred from the challenge. They figured a small scale charter business for the less competitive patrons would work in this area. They secured a small docking space in a marina on the Florida Bay side of the island. The locals were a bit skeptical at first, but were won over by their courage to take on this task. Slider and Darla both had become skilled at "fishing and boatmanship." They lived on the restored Chris Craft at first and once established were able to find a small rental on the island. It resembled a "bunker" part of the build ethic of the Keys to withstand tropical weather. Although small it served the purpose. Business started slowly, but their reserve funds got them through and once word got around they had found a niche. Not everyone wanted a tournament style atmosphere. A relaxing day fishing on the bay with a small group of friends worked for many tourists.

This early morning in late January was on the cool side for the Keys. The bay was calm and the sun had just peaked through. The Stanbridge's, Kevin and Diane, were on a sort of a second honeymoon. Neither fished, but the Plantation Key atmosphere made them feel compelled to try. A far cry from home, Toronto. They were already contemplating retirement, although it was a few years away yet. Definitely looking for a warmer, more laid back location. They found the small charter boat, named Darla's Love, at the end of the dock. Troy was washing down the deck, Darla was in the galley preparing lunch for a party of four. Troy's long hair was pulled back in a ponytail, his full beard specked with grey. He had a cutoff black hoodie, grey cargo shorts and black canvas converse sneaks. He looked up and smiled.

"Come on aboard, we are about ready to push off."

Kevin and Diane carefully boarded, introduced themselves.

"Troy, right, the other couple backed out, afraid of the water, I will pay the fare for them, we still want to go out."

"Hey, no problem, the bay is real calm, we got a few spots where other boats have been having luck, we'll hit um, should be good day."

"Good, we're looking forward to it "

"Usually we go out for 4 hours, we don't have anything booked for the afternoon, so we stay out longer, just let us know how long you want to stay out. Couple of minutes and we will be ready to push off."

Darla stepped up from the galley on to the deck. Her auburn hair was now cut short, covered by a tan bucket hat. She had on light blue fishing shorts, and a plain white long sleeve t shirt that revealed a slight bulge in her belly.

"This is my wife Darla, meet Kevin and Diane. That's all we got today, should be a relaxing day on the bay."

Kevin smiled, "sorry about the other couple, I told Troy, we will cover, um really sorry."

"Hey, don't worry, we can split the extra lunch, my appetite has grown with my belly."

Diane looked her over and smiled, "first one, how far long are you."

"Yeah, four months, a little late in life, but we are good with it, she will be born with sea legs."

Troy put his arm around her and kissed her softly on the mouth, " let's go catch some fish."

Darla reached up, pulled him close, and whispered how much she loved him.

The engines fired and Darla's Love pulled away from the dock and headed slowly out to the bay.

It was cold, lower 40's and overcast, a late January Saturday at the McKinney Equestrian Center. Building two had been set up for a three day dog agility trial. The two horse show rings had been converted to dog agility rings, the equipment set for the various classes and changed as the classes changed. The dirt surface had been graded, but the Friday trial had partially compromised the surface. The Friday entry was light, but Saturday and Sunday had the maximum entry numbers. Dogs were crated all along the outer walls of the facility and the spectators and competitors watched from the metal grandstands adjacent to each ring.

Gar had taken the day off from the ranch, he was now the foreman and ran the operation for the owners. It had been an early morning for both of them, Olivia getting the dogs and herself ready for the trial. Loading up for the 40 minute trip to the center. Her FJ had been replaced with a newer Chevy Tahoe. Steele and JD didn't know the difference, just glad they were along for ride. Gar lived there now, the relationship had blossomed and they were both comfortable with living together and moving forward with their relationship.

Gar sat at the top of the grandstands but was in earshot of two women and a man, all of whom were competitors. They were watching one of the classes they were not entered in. Gar's faded Levis, buffalo plaid flannel shirt, well- worn cowboy boots a bit out of place with the agility crowd. He observed Steele and Olivia staging up at the gate area for their first run of the day.

The three sitting a few rows ahead of him probably didn't notice him, or maybe they did.

"Why do you hate her so much, she is no threat to you, certainly not world team material, that dog, he's not fast enough," the speaker nodded to the other women, a 40 something women dressed in the usual agility garb covered by a World Team jacket.

"I don't know, look at her, killer bod, she never stumbles, always seems so calm, that dog, he's like a robot."

"Yeah, she's pretty, seems self-confident and I got a look at her boyfriend, right off the ranch but good looking in a rough kind of way. I get it."

"Yeah and I understand she has a PI license, calls herself a private investigator. What a joke, comes from Florida, I think."

"Yeah, friend of mine saw her and that dog, at the Invitational a few years ago. Hey come on if you want to be anybody you gotta run a border, or a border mix like you, who would waste their time on that dog, that breed."

The man turned around, from the row ahead of the two women, he caught a glimpse of Gar. Gar was smiling and shaking his head.

He voiced his opinion, "hey have you two ever seen that dog drop a bar, no right, structurally he is probably the best thing here, he always runs hard and rarely screws up, I'll take that any day. They have become a tough team, can get placements on a good day."

The conversation continued, Gar focused on the ring as Olivia and Steele were at the start line. It was a jumper's course, Olivia did a two jump lead out. She had a plain navy hooded sweatshirt, gray sweatpants, Solomon trail runners and covered her head with a black watch cap. It was almost as cold inside as outside. On command Steele took off, they traversed the course with grace and Steele qualified and ran 11 seconds under course time. 11 more MACH points.

Gar met Olivia at the crating area. JD was also entered today in novice and looked up as if to say, is it my turn. Steele settled in the crate and got into his chill mode. He took a quick drink from the water bowl. Olivia hugged Gar, he smiled and gave her a quick kiss on the lips.

"I know this bores you, nice every once in a while for you to watch, I never thought I would be comfortable with it."

"It's going to be a long day, how about we go to dinner after we get home and the dogs are settled."

Olivia flashed a wicked smile, "how about we get the dogs settled and take a nice long hot shower together, and?"

Gar looked her right in the eyes, "sounds good, like you're reading my mind."

"Hey, thanks for coming into my life. The mind reading part I'm working on it. Look watch JD and Steele, I'm going over to the scorer and pick up the qualifying sticker. "

Olivia started to walk away, turned and kissed Gar one more time, walked towards the trial superintendent's office, turned one more time, looked back at Gar and smiled.

About the Author

Kname's Book is James Gregory's debut novel. A retired child abuse investigator, the author and his wife live in North Texas with their two dogs.